Jubilee

Jubilee

The Emancipation
of Life and Love

道

ROB WOMACK

A Publication from
THE QUIET REVOLUTION OF THE HEART

2024

Published by

The Quiet Revolution of the Heart
Durham, North Carolina

© 2024 Rob Womack
All rights reserved
Published 2024
Printed in the United States of America

Book design by Lydia Hall

30 29 28 27 26 25 24   1 2 3 4 5 6 7

ISBN 979-8-9910108-0-1

Library of Congress Control Number: 2024912630

Dedicated to all
who quietly embody kin-dom,
who elucidate Christ-Light,
for all those
who yearn to see,
for all those
who yearn
to Be

Many blessings
to You
and to all those
You Love

Contents

We have inherited many stories
Some have served us worse than others.

What follows is a new addition
to an ancient mythology
of both the sacred and the mundane
transcribed in the voice of a common mystic
rooted in the eternal reality,
from the original to the present,
including how one reckless and
docile species ran so far afoul
and a gentle Prophet's unsettling message
as to how they may yet find their way home.

A work of fiction, like a fable or myth,
which rings eerily truthful.
Each paragraph
a tiny poem
embedded in the long arc of
the story of the cosmos
of who we are,
how we came to be,
and where we might go from here.

A story many hoped would never again be told
and some knew not how long the wait.

My chief desire is to show that what is most mysterious and most exalted is also that which, strangely enough, turns out to be most ordinary and nearest to hand, and that what is most glorious in its transcendence is also that which is humblest in its wonderful immediacy, and that we know far more than we are usually aware of knowing, in large part because we labor to forget what is laid out before us in every moment, and because we spend so much of our lives wondering in dreams, in a deep but fitful sleep.

The Experience of God: Being, Consciousness, Bliss by David Bentley Hart. (Yale University Press, 2013, p. 84)

An Origin Story, Revisited

ooooo

In the beginning, there was Emptiness, the Ineffable. Without name or division, there was neither space nor separation. Hence, no motion or time. Only something like a mustard seed; in size smaller than a grain of salt. If anything existed beforehand, scientists and theologians would agree: So far beyond human comprehension, It should be considered meaningless. What came afterwards would seem utterly miraculous, if not for the fact that It was also the natural order of the universe unfurling before our very eyes.

Bound within the speck of a tiny seed was a trinity of all Matter, Energy, and Instruction floating amid the Nameless. Every molecule, every photon, every organizing principle, for all time, compressed in a single unified Seed: Destined to become, someday in the future, the infinite universe.

For clarity going forward, let *Matter* be a word to represent Energy bound in a knot. *Energy* then represents the threads which weave a vast cosmic cloth. *Instruction*, in turn, must represent the principles which choreograph interactions of Matter and Energy, of particles and waves, respectively.

In waves, Energy moves through the warp and woof of an interconnected universe. Knots of potential Energy may, at times, act more as particles than as waves. None of whom are too large nor too small to be moved regardless of the Name. At certain energetic frequencies, even the Ineffable can be felt, touched, and swayed. Everything flows responsively within the intricate dance of an infinite Universe.

For a brief moment in time, long before such concepts were yet to be imagined, (Or longer? Who knows? Only the Ineffable was there to bear witness) the density of a tiny seed pulled inward so tightly, complete stillness was achieved. Then, inexplicably, Instructions embedded in the tiny seed ordered a direct about-face. Energy converted from inward pull to outward push. Matter moved. Did the seed slowly, or rapidly, wobble, vibrate, or spin? Did momentum build to such velocity that mutual attraction was completely overwhelmed? Or rather, did the Emptiness simply yield and release? Did the space beyond so relax that barriers collapsed and existence found itself lacking any constraints?

Regardless, an event occurred which scientists from a distant vista would dub the Big Bang. Such a name only led to further questions: Was it, as its name implies, sudden and violent? Like an intense burst of aerosol spray? Or more like a bubble which gradually expands until, too thin to hold together any longer, splits into innumerable smaller versions, fractals, of itself? Or instead, has it split at all? Might the seed be expanding reality into Emptiness as it grows? Any memories have long since faded into the mist. The images chosen are mere metaphors left to imaginations of Beings, like you and me, also known as *us*.

Though a layperson, and more mystic than theologian or scientist at that, I perceive the mustard seed, as you may too, as the Original Source at a point of midoscillation—like a wave or a respiration. The tiny mustard seed in a moment of utmost density, of utter stillness, represents the completion of a deep inhale; the pause when the diaphragm holds for an exchange of give and receive, but on a cosmic scale. We live through the long exhale.

The emerging universe has been dancing like a rippling wave ever since. Slowly expanding through the spiral and swirl; rotate, orbit, and collide; coalesce, collapse, and repeat. This era of the dance has been continuous for 13.5 billion Earth-years. Thus far, and thankfully still counting, that is. Due to the universe's ongoing expansion, and at an accelerating pace no less, we may deduce that the present moment we occupy is still early in the long exhale. Which is to say, time is in our favor.

The long exhale stretches the universe farther and farther from Center. As it does, the units of time, space, distance, and speed, by their very nature, morph in due measure. Though the metrics in the universal dance continuously change, one infant species, in one brief era, on one remote planet, attempts to rigidly define all understanding. If their gaze gently softened, what else might they see?

First, behold the tiny mustard seed. Our Greatest Great-Grandparent, the Source from which all seeds emerge. It is One. It is Whole. It is Shalom. Let us date this earliest ancestor, representing the fullness of all space and time, in more manageable increments, as a percentage, or a century, aged 100 units of time.

In early childhood, development was prodigious. A single seed of intensely compressed energy reversed course to outwardly unfurl galaxy upon galaxy. Within time's first seven increments, as many as 200 billion galaxies formed within the observable regions of limitless space. One of the many, later named the Milky Way, is itself composed of 100 billion suns. Within its constellations, without exaggeration, orbit an equal number of planets. Maybe more. One among them, our most beloved, pulls us close to its inner core.

The pace and breadth of such change in a minute span of time is quite staggering. A fundamental principle of the unified universe may thus be inferred: Within a single thread of continuity, the waves of potential for change are nearly unimaginable. Possibilities would seem truly miraculous, if not plainly visible to the spirit's eye.

After the first seven units of time, its work seemingly complete, our Greatest Great-Grandparent paused for a period of deep rest. The Sabbath lasted quite a long time. Not until the age of 66 ¾ units did another meaningful event transpire. It, the Ineffable, was well past middle age when, in the expansive skies, a watery globe coalesced.

Such a long delay would indicate nothing fundamental or inevitable in the principles of the universe.

The late-blooming planet might be a mere accident, hardly a manifested destiny. Although always a possibility, it was one among many realized. Due to the planet's actual existence, its presence may at least be judged as well within the margins of probability. This unnamed planet, later to be called *Earth*, might be one random element among innumerable others. Or a singularly unique event within the magnificent cosmic dance.

Furthermore, such an event could be cherished as a rare and precious gift. Or, on the other hand, it could be received as an unwelcome surprise: For instance, as an innkeeper might greet a family of wayward migrants—one clearly expecting a child, and it illegitimate, no less. (Such an atrocious pronoun and adjective to ascribe to a child.) "No vacancy here. I'm sorry. We don't serve your kind. Out in the stable the animals do just fine on nights colder than this."

An unwelcome guest to mistreat, neglect, or abuse? Or a precious gift to nurture and to love as if At-One with you? The chosen images and interpretations seem to hold great bearing on the ways in which we proceed. Therefore, a second fundamental principle can be deduced: Instructions embedded in the mustard seed must have given options to express, later dubbed the *responsibility and freedom to choose.*

Almost immediately, our youngest great-grandparent, the newborn planet without a name, was adopted by a star. In elongated loops, they began circling. As a result, upon the planet, warmth ebbed and flowed with cold.

Seasons blended one into the next. The tiny planet, as if on a spindle, spun rapidly with excitement. The sun rose. The sun set. Day blended with night.

Closer to the surface, conditions were not so orderly. Silence was regularly punctuated by lightning's snap. Sunlight was often obscured by clouds of darkness. Winds swirled into vortices. Nights flashed ominously. The crust oozed red lava and spewed malodorous gas. The planet was truly a hot mess.

In the vicinity, debris sailed to and fro. If trajectories intersected, an ambush descended on the vulnerable planet. One collision landed with such a punch, the spindle tilted twenty-three degrees off-center. North and south were never quite the same. From that day forward, winter here, summer there. Days stretched forth. Then contracted. Yet another strike dislodged a chunk and flung it high above. As if tethered by an invisible cord, the mercurial moon hovered near its origin. Ever faithful to the sun, it played hide and seek with Mother.

As cosmic debris repeatedly collided with the watery planet, divots emptied again and again of waters as broad as seas. With a gargantuan splash, dust and steam arose, interrupting skies drenched in sun. Lighter elements hovered aloft. An anaerobic atmosphere swaddled the newborn planet. Heavier elements fell in sheets of liquid rain. Seas and oceans gathered once again. The high ground was tamped and fortified with minerals and vitamins.

In spite of the harsh collisions, the orbiting pair appeared quite pliable. From a distance, the two became beautifully rounded globes. Like droplets of oil in water, the moon and planet seem to be pulled inward from an equalizing Center. Or another possibility: Maybe they were smoothed, from the outside in, as the gentle touch of a Potter's fingers molds clay on a spinning wheel.

Such beautiful perfection, however, is a sly conceit. The presence of liquid water, evenly spread by gravity, hides many blemishes. Over the planet's battered surface, from the highest peak to the deepest crevice, is a range of 65,000 feet. If situated side by side, the descent would be twelve miles deep. Sometimes the world differs profoundly from the ways which we perceive.

Eventually, airborne collisions occurred less often. Storms calmed. Stillness settled over the water and the land. As it did, the processes of Life began. In less time required for the universe to assume its expansive shape, processes initiated which culminated in this present moment, and us as participants. No memory was retained, nor does a record exist, of how the processes began. Speculations have been reduced to subjective explanations of well-crafted theories and myths. Here are two examples to help to understand.

Certain imaginations, none of whom were present at the time, view Life as perfect at conception. Perfection soon fell, however, and was forever lost. The Creator gave Adam breath, Eve a rib, before handing her off to her husband for life. Unfortunately for the newlyweds, the Creator looked away or dozed off. One cunning, disobedient snake slipped into the garden and spoke to two naively obedient listeners. A single flaw was the source of humanity's downfall for eternity. Many a neighbor has suffered the consequence. The rest, as they say, is dismissed as history: For better or for worse, what you see is what you get.

Rather than Adam, but in a strikingly similar tone, some imaginations suggest Life branched from one last unified common ancestor. With less creativity, the ancestor was named LUCA. She is the last known point from which all living Beings diverge and ascend. Such a theory, however, fails to integrate the convergence and cooperation of interconnected Beings with no hierarchical rank or order.

Though attributes of how and why are explained subjectively, descriptions of when can be grounded in hard evidence. In the planet's earliest rotations around the sun, almost immediately on a cosmic scale, impressions were made which resemble the cells of Life as seen today. The markers are dated to the fifth increment of time following the planet's chance formation.

These earliest indications of Life were found in fossilized rocks like thumbprints impressed upon geologic tombstones. The marks were located in far-flung places now known as Australia, Africa, and Greenland. The evidence, however, may be circumstantial. The weight of physical objects leaves distinct impressions. In contrast, like waves or wind, the animating energy of spiritual consciousness leaves less than a wisp.

From the Big Bang to LUCA, or Adam unto Eve, beginnings are assumed to begin in a singularity. And yet, what is most meaningful exists in relationships of pairs and groups. Since these disparate stories seem inherently narrow, imperfect, and incomplete, might there be a Third Way? Let's see.

As the watery globe coalesced, Instructions coded in the tiny mustard seed almost immediately generated five processes for Life's incarnation. For ease of translation, these five are known as cellular formation, autocatalysis, homeostasis, adaptive replication, and metabolism. The processes, in all likelihood, began concurrently. Diversity followed by convergence is far less time-consuming than a linear sequence of new grafting onto old hierarchically. From the outset, convergence instilled interdependence of cooperative relationships, and afterwards, symbiosis. Later known as *Life*.

Because Life circulates as particles of Matter, and the animating energy we call Love radiates in waves, because neither can manifest without the cooperative symbiosis of the other, what appear as two are here joined as One. Henceforth they unite as *Life and Love*. The phenomenon described may be known by another, more familiar name: *God*. Merely two linguistic symbols for one reality.

One of Life and Love's Instructions, called cell formation, may have begun at the edges where two inhospitable environments meet. In the tumultuous conditions of the unnamed planet, edges blended to form niches. For instance, deep in the oceans' depths, hot gas emerged from the ocean floor. It blended with cold water descending from above. Where the hot gas and cold liquid met, a niche was formed. Likewise, imagine a shore where water laps over land. As tides recede, a niche emerges in shallow pools left behind.

At these marginal edges, where differences overlap, material elements assembled a porous boundary to separate inside from out. The tiny refuge allowed exchange with, and safety from, unpredictable conditions outside. A stable container provided consistency for the inner workings of Life and Love.

Lipids, more commonly known as fat molecules, may have been among the first to circle the wagons and form cells. Lipids, by temperament, are quite unique. One half of the molecule clings to water. The other half avoids. Together, they are insoluble. In wet environments, they assume the shape of a sphere, like a moon, planet, or star. Within the spherical refuge, water is safely harbored from the thirsty atmosphere.

If the age and spread of geographic tombstones are any indication, the earliest cells formed quickly and concurrently. They drew on a variety of methods and materials in a multitude of diverse environments. Therefore, the formation of stable containers in unstable conditions may yet be another principle operating within the natural order of the universe. For simplicity, allow stability, care, and protection to be subsumed within the fundamental principle herein named: *Continuity in the midst of change.*

Like the walls of a home, or the fabric of our clothes, as well as the skin they shelter, the microscopic cells which comprise each of the above could be fractals of the principle at work. To be otherwise exposed and unprotected, prone to the dangers outside, would leave Beings literally turned inside out.

As physical cells played with various methods, other processes practiced their emerging roles. Based on Instructions echoing from the tiny mustard seed, certain prominent elements performed a dance later called *autocatalysis*. As a result, these elements were able to join, separate, and reconstitute. Such a process allows for longevity in the midst of instability; again, continuity in the midst of change.

Imagine a compound molecule, such as yourself, whose external conditions change. An event occurs: Another molecule is encountered. Without affinity, prejudice, or malice, the first is profoundly altered. It literally comes apart. Embedded within the scattered elements, somehow the wisdom seems intrinsic. Like magic, or a miracle, in a series of transformative steps, the original compound returns to itself unharmed. Healing follows adversity. What was once whole, could be broken, and find its way to wholeness again.

Indeed, compound molecules discovered what was once divided could return to wholeness—and be doubled. The process of autocatalysis, initially beginning with One, could bring into existence duplicates. Emanating from a continuity now called *heredity*, replication was possible. Not only that, but the molecules also discovered an ability to alter incrementally. After many revolutions, and much practice, patience, and persistence, autocatalysis learned to replicate and adapt. A learning process capable of change, incorporating death, and striving for perpetuity, would later be called *evolution*.

As its name implies, autocatalysis is a process of self-(re)generation. The process may also be a precursor to homeostasis—a term which describes the tendency for a cell, and systems of cells, to flexibly maintain internal stability in the midst of surrounding change. Two terms, homeostasis and evolution, describe the tendency to protect and maintain Life as well as the Beings who comprise it. The former in the immediacy of the day-to-day. The latter for perpetuity.

Had life been so unfortunate as to manifest itself in a perfected state, even a slight variation in external conditions may have tolled its death knell. Instead, as mercurial conditions outside shifted, Life and Love flexibly adjusted. Mutations allowed the processes of life, like their offspring, to learn, adapt, diversify, and proliferate. Lessons hard won? Some, yes. But, to the third and fourth generation, forever worthwhile.

Many adaptations incorporated by Life and Love were unequivocally neutral. They neither extended nor shortened, added to nor took away from longevity. Qualitatively beautiful and blessed, Life and Love creates playful diversity rather than a final solution for the singular best. It is a process which seeks to lengthen the lives of many, not to perfect the few. For those with ears to hear, and eyes to see, the evidence abounds.

If a neutral variation happened to associate with Beneficence, far and wide it spread. Beneficence was naturally selected and cumulatively multiplied. It fostered Life and Love and lengthened longevity. Such a statement may seem tautological because goodness and care are so plainly evident as is water to the fish and the forest to a tree.

Maleficence, on the other hand, aims to kill before it dies. Rather than diversify and integrate, it stifles. It eradicates. It attempts to consume without limit. Maleficence destroys in a relative instant, because it cannot love throughout time. It is like an unquenchable cup filled to overflowing. Eventually it gurgles and drowns in its own toxicity.

Maleficence is naturally deselected because it inhibits Life and Love. That which causes harm is bound to disappear. Branches which prove themselves incompatible, those that stifle others, inevitably wither or rot. Fortunately, for us, Maleficence does not instantaneously combust. To evolve, Life and Love yields with patience. It awaits change, hopeful for learning and adaptation. Reconciliation is much preferred over elimination. Beneficence, like Life and Love, is destined to thrive. This too is a fundamental principle embedded in the Instructions echoing throughout the universe.

As cell formation and autocatalysis developed, other activities were underway nearby. Whereas in some encounters compounds learned to separate, replicate, and reconfigure, in others two met and merged. At first, contact was entirely random. Soft, round bodies with no appendage could only lazily drift and hope for chance encounters. As amorphous hosts became more plentiful and concentrated, opportunities improved. Upon contact, like a hospitable host, one would open and welcome a surprise visitor.

Eventually, the amorphous hosts met partners of unusual shapes and merged specialties and skills. Mutual interdependence generated synergy. Symbiosis followed. For example, neighbors of various shapes generated motion with their bodies to push, rotate, or sway. The roomy, oblong host sensed they were being propelled ahead. Other neighbors, differently shaped, attached to the bow rather than the stern. Like arms widespread, they reached out to draw others in. Where two or more were gathered to work cooperatively, opportunities for survival, replication, and longevity soon followed.

Not long thereafter, they discovered the cooperative arrangements worked too well. Not every ounce drawn inward was useful to consume. Indeed, unused substances, if allowed to accumulate, were quite toxic for cellular bodies to hold. Therefore, on the front end, symbiotic hosts and partners learned to act with self-restraint. Consumption became selective. On the back end, if you will, receivers learned to release and pass along.

Components expelled by one were abundantly well-suited for their neighbors' consumption. This allowed accumulations to dissipate and extended the longevity of everyone. Like weaves in a braid, the sequencing fostered interdependence and mutual flourishing. Each assumed their role to nurture a neighbor's well-being. The space they inhabited was becoming organized, balanced, and self-sustaining, later called a *system*.

Within the process now known as metabolism, proto-Beings learned to limit what was taken in. A complete minimum was most beneficial, for them as well as neighbors nearby. By living within limits, the integrated body participated in a practice of self-regulation, later called *self-expression* and *freedom and responsibility*. The cells' internal integrity was harmoniously maintained alongside the external environment composed of neighbors nearby.

Concurrently, nature's elements were being assembled into complex arrangements. A patient practice of assimilating simplicity into complexity bonded the four elements most plentiful: hydrogen, oxygen, carbon, and nitrogen. These four combined with phosphorous to generate peptides. Peptides extended the practice and arranged themselves into the more complex nucleic acids. Nucleic acids stepped it up a notch and assembled deoxyribonucleic acid. Better known by the acronym DNA, this compound material was destined to become a preferred carrier for instructions in heredity and replication.

In other developments nearby, the four most prevalent elements combined, but partnered with sulfur instead. Amino acids were formed. Amino acids bonded together in more complex strands later called *proteins*. Proteins compose the structure and scaffolding of the physical-material bodies known as *Beings*. In diverse arrangements of the most common elements, Instructions from the Greatest Great-Grandparent were embroidering the threads for a vast and living web.

The concurrent processes organizing symbiotic life soon overlapped. Instructions choreographing interactions of Matter and Energy performed a magical leap. When matter learned to absorb solar energy, a new equilibrium was achieved. The spinning planet jettisoned into live animation. During the period of Life's conception, our youngest great-grandparent, the unnamed planet, was itself quite young. In less than five units of time after the infant planet coalesced, Life and Love had found a toehold and has yet to release.

Of all Beings identified, one of the first, the oldest thus far, has existed for twenty-six units of time; one quarter of the age of the entire universe in its current oscillation. Our oldest grandparent was named neither Adam, nor Eve, nor LUCA, but Cyanobacteria. Cyano was among the first to merge the processes to metabolize energy, adapt, reproduce, and die. The earliest Beings were the simplest and, by no coincidence, the most resilient, it seems.

After Cyano's period of gestation a second season of Sabbath ensued. For twenty-two units of time, Life and Love took a break from diverse proliferation to hone its basic craft. During the rehearsals, some notable adaptations emerged. Cyano was so prolific, its exhalations altered the anaerobic atmosphere. The skies were supplemented, one part in five, with oxygen. As a result, the planet became more hospitable for the future offspring who rely on oxygen to survive.

During this same period, some cells diverged from Cyano and adopted an identity of their own. They integrated something like a cell within a cell. One wed with another in a symbiotic relationship. The cell within was later given a name, *nucleus*. Contained within the nuclei were the nucleic acids which would come to such prominence. The complex strands of DNA and RNA contained therein encoded amino acids to form proteins. Furthermore, by way of DNA's memory and instructions, proteins organized into physical bodies and united with the energetic-spiritual conscious to animate them.

Through studious practice and mastery, nucleated cells also developed organelles called *mitochondria*. Within the cell, mitochondria transform energy acquired from sources outside. Then, in an act of mutual reciprocity, they redistribute energy to animate the host.

The process by which mitochondria developed must be common to us all. Every cell which contains a nucleus, from the simplest to the most complex, also contains mitochondria. Whether nuclei and mitochondria were developed by mergers and acquisitions, or as proprietary innovations, no one quite recalls. Events and processes leave behind few imprints, and even fewer explanations. If Life were represented as a tree, Cyanobacteria would occupy a ramifying root, but mitochondria and nuclei would be integral with the trunk. They join the interconnected branches above to a shared history, a mysterious story, of common origins.

In spite of the aforementioned theories and myths, in all likelihood our ancestry did not originate from one Being distinct and unique. Certainly not one literally raised from mud, wind, and bone. Odds are much more in favor of a convergence of diverse material and energetic processes animated by spiritual consciousness. As is Mystery's tendency, it may seem paradoxical: Life and Love is simplicity embedded in complexity, resiliency woven from fragility, continuity in the midst of change.

Also during the second Sabbath, some cells diverged to form another unique identity. They retained the mitochondria and stayed close to the family. But within the porous boundary, a close cousin was fostered, a unique organelle later called *chloroplasts*. In a stroke of genius, chloroplasts learned to bypass the intermediaries. Like their ancestors of old, they relearned the ability to absorb energy directly from the sun. Chloroplasts assumed the roles of energy transformation as well as the synthesis of proteins and nucleic acids. With the step towards multi-purpose generalist, they became slightly more independent. To state this somewhat differently, the more specialization within a system, the more interdependent the Beings.

During the ninety-fifth increment of time, the second Sabbath drew to its conclusion and Life and Love's diverse proliferation began in earnest. Right away, cells began to mimic the resonating patterns of Life and Love. They combined into more complex, intimate, and symbiotic relationships. Multicellular Beings emerged. Almost immediately, in the increments of the universe, a lineage of photosynthetic Beings, better known as *plants*, developed. Soon thereafter, other multicellular Beings, better known as *animals*, arose. The younger animals are directly dependent, within one or two degrees, on the presence of their elders: living, breathing plants. Plants gather the sun so food can be shared, and, in long exhalations, they cleanse the oxygenated atmosphere.

Without plants, the existence of many neighbors would suddenly cease. The least resilient would quickly die of asphyxiation. The few who managed to catch a breath would succumb more slowly to starvation. Therefore, neighbors wisely and carefully nurtured the habitats of plants as if they were a beloved neighbor's home. At one time it was commonly known: If the lives of plants grow long and prosper, their dependents grow more robust as well.

As with the accretion of the planet, so may it be with the presence of the multicellular Beings. Emerging so slowly, so late in the long arc of the universe, rather than destiny, they may be little more than another possibility realized. Their apparent abundance on the unnamed planet may reveal only a short-term phenomenon like flecks of grass which wither in a season.

For a brief moment, let us entertain a more appealing narrative: Life, and its indivisible symbiotic companion Love, could paradoxically be both fundamental and unique. Unique because, though it is possible that

Life has arisen and faded repeatedly throughout the seasons of time, from our current vantage point only one small sample remains. From here, we see no other planetary Beings with which to compare. For all intents and purposes, we might be a once-in-a-lifetime cosmic event of infinite preciousness; a rare, singular moment in the eternal dance of the Source some call God.

Likewise fundamental because, just as embedded Instructions manage interactions of all Matter and Energy, we too are clearly woven into the fabric of the universe. We are here. We exist. We are one element in the long exhalation of the presently expanding universe. We are Breath. We are Spirit. We are the distant, interconnected great-grandchildren of One Ancient Seed.

In either case, fundamental or unique, as threads within a web, we are indubitably beholden to care well for our elders, neighbors, siblings, and kin including their habitats of soil, water, and air. Everything, including each other, including ourselves. Life and Love, and the Beings made manifest, could be a precious gift. In which case, we are simultaneously both the givers and receivers as well as the gift itself. Life and Love's overarching purpose, for all participants, may be to extend the gift far into perpetuity.

Sadly, the vision of one late arrival became occluded as if a plank had lodged in one of their green, green eyes. They lost the ability to take a perspective other than their own. For example, the gift described above was read as if the pronoun "we" referred to them exclusively. When, in fact, "we" includes us *all*.

The late arrivals had neither the experience nor maturity to witness, much less comprehend, the Greatest Great-Grandparent's long history. Though newborn infants on the unnamed planet, they began to think of themselves as more than just unique. They lauded themselves, among all others, as ultimate, as supreme; an incredulous notion, previously unheard of in the entirety of the universe.

With this in mind and spirit, let us proceed with patience and humility. Following the Way, we may soon discover from where they diverged and the Middle Path to return to Jubilee.

In the indigenous view, humans are viewed as somewhat lesser beings in the democracy of species. We are referred to as the younger brothers of Creation, so like younger brothers we must learn from our elders. Plants were here first and have had a long time to figure things out. They live both above and below ground and hold the earth in place. Plants know how to make food from light and water. Not only do they feed themselves, but they make enough to sustain the lives of all the rest of us. Plants are providers for the rest of the community and exemplify the virtue of generosity, always offering food.

Braiding Sweetgrass by Robin Wall Kimmerer. (Milkweed Editions, 2013, p. 346)

Tamers of Fire

ooooo

We have arrived at the ninety-ninth increment of time. On the far horizon, the tiny mustard seed hovers; now barely a glimmer in our Greatest Great-Grandparent's eye. In the opposite direction lies our future destination: The present moment awaits. Relatively speaking, closer than ever, yet still quite a long distance away. Solid ground is barely distinguishable from murky sky. Surroundings seem vaguely familiar as if at any moment a twinge of déjà vu may flutter. To focus our attention, the aperture gradually hones in to reframe time's narrative arc. We gaze across units of time, from here forward, fractional in size.

Near the midpoint of this ninety-ninth increment, something akin to six months ago, an asteroid slammed into the unnamed planet like a cue ball on the break. The impact was nearly a direct hit, a mere twenty-one degrees off-center of the equatorial line. An ominous cloud of ash, dust, and vapor ascended skyward. Like an enormous blanket it unfurled to insulate surface from sun. A shadow was cast far and wide from sea to darkened sea.

With the sun's light so thoroughly obscured, many plants could not survive. Many animals, as predicted, perished alongside. No one left standing stopped to count. From a distant vista, one species estimated that three-fourths of the living breathed their last. Fortunately, a remnant refused to acquiesce. Tightly to the threads they clung to (re)weave the web: the web of Life and Love.

The remnant, in all likelihood, did not include our youngest grandparent, Primate, though the timing of their emergence remains unclear. No geologic tombstones have been located to indicate their presence prior to impact. The earliest remains found thus far came to rest not long thereafter. From the point of impact to the time of our youngest grandparent's earliest death elapsed eleven million Earth-years.

If, however, our youngest grandparent was among the survivors, and had indeed emerged prior to collision, their time had been short. Genetic tests estimate one-sixth of a unit, a mere two months in the fractional increments of the universe. When the shock waves settled and the skies darkened, Primate was in their infancy. With no points of comparison, the extreme abnormality would surpass all understanding. Experiences of darkness and hunger would seem normal, immutable, ordained.

If the latter scenario was historical, our youngest grandparents' ability to withstand grave hardship would be indubitable. However, if the hard evidence holds up, and they arose after the skies had cleared, and have remained as such ever since, the resilience of the offspring of our youngest grandparent would also remain unclear.

When sunnier skies did appear, Life and Love's Instructions for the interactions of Matter and Energy resumed almost instantly. It happened so quickly, in fact, that the free expression of this divine mystery would seem a fundamental principle operating within the effervescent universe.

As Life and Love's artful play resumed, new shapes and colors coalesced among the resilient remnant. In the unfurling, new varieties of plants developed to absorb the sun and cleanse the atmosphere. New varieties of animals emerged to cull the fruit, harvest the sun, and return dust into dust. Animals died naturally to feed the fungi connecting tree root to tree root. Their nutritious remains seeped slowly upward from spongy soil to sun-drenched treetops. New fruit ripened into expectant nuts and seeds to wed with the Wind and the Beings who carry them. Ancestor into offspring, new life into life.

Life and Love played with creative variety gently and slowly. Many adaptations proved beneficial to the health and longevity of all interdependent Beings. Colorful varieties, both neutral and beneficial, proliferated here and yon. On the other hand, a few changes induced harm to worsen health and shorten life. Effects rippled outward similarly. The interdependent web of Life and Love shares in consequences equally. Rain falls on the just and unjust alike. Fortunately, homeostasis insists that harmful mutations are not allowed to forever run amok. Maleficence inevitably leads to die offs. The greater the overabundance, the harsher the collapse. During the descent, equilibrium is restored. Progressive balance is the perpetual norm.

Among those eating the replenished fruit of the vine were offspring with wombs and spines, known as *mammals* and *vertebrates* in this day and time. Among the burgeoning life was our youngest grandparent named, in hindsight, *Primate*. Such an odd name for one so late to the game. According to the evidence, as mentioned above, they only emerged around mid-August of the ninety-ninth increment of time. The name, like a monument, however, grants a status un-earned. One might be led to believe they were the first, or uppermost, of a kind.

The elders had survived five mass extinctions and adapted to new conditions. By way of these adapta-tions, their offspring had sufficiently differentiated and adopted a new identity. Subsequently, the offspring of Primates would be grouped and divided into more fa-miliar names such as gorillas, chimpanzees, and orang-utans. Soon they would diverge yet again and acquire a new name, *humans*.

Like many of their land-bound neighbors, Primate used four appendages for stability and propulsion across uneven ground. Over time, however, variations began to appear. Physical changes were visible to the naked eye. Subsequent changes, though hidden from sight, would be clearly visible to the attentive mind.

The changes allowed some Primates to stand heads above the rest. A few were born differently angled at the juncture of the hips. The strange new pelvis allowed them to stop and stand upright for several minutes at a time. With this new flexibility, front legs were freed for an unconventional use. While in motion, they still navigated forward direction, but when stationary, they could reach into branches overhead. Appendages were freed to gather Life and Love and bring It into our inner core.

When ordinary neighbors came upon fruit beyond the reach of short necks and jaws, they could do nothing more than stare hungrily with despair. Primates with the unusual gait, on the other hand, used front paws and gravity to haphazardly club fruit to the ground. The object of their fascination now within reach, all of the Primates could sit and comfortably eat.

In normal seasons, the alteration of hips, spines, and legs held no disadvantage or benefit. Young Primates had no prejudice against difference. When sun mixed with rain, low-hanging fruit proved abundant. Those who held fast to the ground as well as those with the unusual gait found fruit sufficient for their needs.

However, when the balance of light to water dipped, low-hanging fruit did not ripen normally. Those who lacked the ability to roam far, or gather from above, could not as easily survive the extremes. Death nibbled first at the margins; then, crept inward. Those loved the most, the very old and the very young, were often the first ones claimed. Beings who embodied the wisdom of the past, as well as those responsible to carry it on, were fungi's first meals. Ancestor into offspring, tree root to tree root, ashes to ashes, dust to dust. Sorrow was abundant when the fruit withered, but the balance of Energy to Matter, Being to Being, always remained.

Fortunately for later generations, less visible changes were taking shape in the spirit-minds of Primates with an unusual gait. Unique abilities of the physical body allowed for changes in behavior as well. Those who could eat the low-hanging fruit or the fruit overhead had options from which to choose. Thus, they had the opportunity to learn to share.

In seasons of plenty, fruit on the branches above was left for the Beings with wings. In seasons of scarcity, a portion from above augmented the meager harvest below. Fruit was divided evenly among everyone. No one consumed more than their minimal needs. Hence, no one had to sacrifice; the system did not suffer. The trees flourished and in subsequent seasons, abundant fruit was restored. Death was kept at bay. In seasons normal and extreme, appetites were voluntarily restrained.

Such attentive cooperation happened so seamlessly, without debate or deliberation, consider it a manifestation of the natural order of the universe. Just as the processes of Life and Love merged into single-cell forebears; just as single cells converged into symbiotic multicellular Beings; just as multicellular Beings organized into interconnected, ecological systems, acts of cooperation seem to be embedded in the Instructions flowing from the Greatest Great-Grandparent. From simplicity, complexity converges; again an echo of continuity in the midst of change.

Due to the benefits of standing upright, reaching out, and learning to share, opportunities to gather the fruit of the vine proliferated alongside longevity. Through practice and repetition, Primate learned other new behaviors as well. Rather than clubbing the fruit with one wild, dominant hand, Primates with the unusual gait discovered two paws cupped together could select one fruit at a time. Its time in the sun preserved, unripened fruit was not wasted. Fruit could be shared with the future, when its rightful time had come. A conservative harvest led to patience and gratitude. Selectivity increased Primates' longevity as well as that of their neighbors who also shared in the fruit of the vine.

As diets improved and life lengthened, Primates with the unusual gait began to notice other physical changes as well. For example, as arms extended, the muscles of the neck, spine, and shoulders stretched to allow one appendage to reach higher in the branches overhead. Alas, at that asymmetric angle, the opposite paw was unable to pair with its mate.

Primate came to learn that disparate objects could perform in new and cooperative ways. Unable to grasp with two paws, Primate began to use two adjacent toes. The higher they stretched, the longer the toes grew. The more frequent the practice, the more nimble too.

Season after season, eventually, front toes lost their identity. They weren't quite themselves anymore. A new name was ascribed: *fingers*.

The ancestors' front appendages had but a single use: to guide and propel mobility. Two blunt objects had gained in versatility and added ten fine instruments. Nimble fingers finessed the details, enabled more selective pruning, and expanded a colorful menu. With two or three fingertips, a diverse variety of small fruits, nuts, and seeds were now available for the choosing. When delicate fingers felt fruit was too young, it could be left safely attached. Days of optimal ripeness lay ahead. A deferred harvest of gratification prospered alongside less waste.

The more diversified and stable their diets became, the healthier Primates remained. In the first place, bodies were better able to avoid illness and injury. If illness or injury did appear, recovery was more expeditious. Excess energy was not necessary to digress from health to illness and then return to baseline contentment. The sun's energy was used more efficiently for the inner adaptations of learning and the outward acts of loving care.

As consumption of the sun's energy from the fruit of the vine became more reliable, internal sensations long felt but largely ignored became distinctly more noticeable. Some sensations seemed to beckon Primate's body to draw nearer. Others of a differing hue wrenched their bodies back. The sensations were like an internal elbow gently nudging to approach or avoid.

A few examples may help. Certain insects, mush-rooms, and overripe fruits raised internal alarms. Fear or disgust pulled Primate back from potential harm. Other fruits, perfectly ripened, elicited waves of delicious delight. If separated from someone deeply loved, or when very lost, a confused sadness emerged. In spirit and mind, and at times physically, they sought to reconnect with the familiar and beloved. If reunited, loved ones groomed, soothed, and cuddled each other. A restful bliss ensued. Any lingering gaps of separation were soon closed.

Primates noticed these same sensations were felt not only within them, but by many of their neighbors as well. Bees on spring's yellow flowers were seen in states of inebriated bliss. Pairs of butterflies were ensconced in a joyful dance. Likewise, flocks of birds at dusk swirled in vivid murmurations; schools of fish swam with mindful ease in unison. The setting sun, an illuminated cloud, and the rolling stream all held passersby in awe and reverence.

Furthermore, Primate observed that what was felt by one affected the feelings of another. Sometimes in equal and at other times opposite ways. When Primate assisted a neighbor in distress, both expressed a sigh of relief, and an ounce of gratitude. Neighbors sampling delectable fruits shifted from bliss to fear when intercepted by Primate's hungry fingers. Some insects in flight seemed stubbornly attracted to Primate and their summer-soaked skin. Until, of course, Primate briskly swatted at them. Message received: "That's too close. Seek your dinner elsewhere."

Our youngest grandparent took note of the sensations felt, those within as well as those of others. Primate could distinguish the sensations as they were being experienced. What had happened out there clearly stirred something in here. Associations between the external and internal coalesced. The interconnections and dynamism of relationships were becoming clear.

Emotions, as they were later known, assisted in the ability to gain perspective, their own as well as that of others, alike and unlike themselves. Primate developed an understanding, later named *empathy*, of the relationships between internal sensations and external events. By way of emotions, they also realized, along with options—to take or to leave, to give or to share, to live or to die—all Beings held preferences to express. *All*, including themselves.

As feelings deepened, memories were more easily retained. Patterns took shape upon the mental maps of the mind. Emotions enhanced learning. Intelligence had been born. Even more importantly, Primate was aware, everyone was here together. No one was alone.

Primate began to observe other aspects of the world around. For example, they noticed some events repeat. Some in cycles short and quick like day alternates with night. Others occurred more slowly. Over many nights, the moon swelled from slivered crescent to full, fecund roundness. Then, just as slowly, it would recess into shadow. The next night it playfully peeked around from the other side of darkness.

The longest cycles followed the sun as it traversed horizons. At its peak, the sun drew a magical arch tall and wide across the sky. Days were long and bright. Nights were terse, but rather warm. At high noon, shadows were nowhere to be found. At its trough, like a low-slung bridge, the sun stayed close to the horizon. As it spanned winter's solemn river, it joined the banks of east and west across a slate gray southern sky.

Like the objects overhead, and the seasons they imparted, the elders, neighbors, siblings, and kin also adhered to cyclical patterns. Between the short cycles of the sun's rise and descent, most rose to work and to play. As the sun departed, they withdrew in gratitude for rest. While Primates were tucked safely in their shelters, neighbors cloaked in darkness foraged through the vacated spaces.

In longer cycles, Primate observed a few neighbors saunter by with their backs turned towards the sun. Some traveled by air, others on hoof. Then as the cycle revolved, the same neighbors returned. This time their faces resplendent in the sun.

The longer they lived and observed, the more clearly the patterns of regularity emerged. With such patterns in mind, Primate noticed they were better equipped to predict what might happen next. As predictions were paired with felt-sensations, they could better discern if what lay ahead was hoped for and preferred, or not. Familiarity and predictable patterns led to better decisions for experiences of safety, health, and peaceful contentedness.

Safety, health, and contentment created a baseline from which to explore curiosity. As neighbors wandered by, Primate ambled alongside, yet not so close as to intrude upon a neighbor's privacy. In the early days, Primate followed only as far as their eyes kept sight of home. From that distance, they promptly returned. During the infancy of intelligence, curiosity led; confidence soon followed.

As fields and paths became more familiar, Primate sensed further could they roam. They might wander out of sight and still find their way home. They began to take exploratory risks and trust in outcomes unknown. Much like cautious neighbors on migration, if landmarks in the mind's eye were strung together, like breadcrumbs on a string, a safe return was nearly guaranteed. Upon arrival, they sensed accomplishment and relief. In vibrant swaths, curiosity and confidence began to bloom almost simultaneously.

As they roamed, mental maps were being drawn and stored of the physical spaces around. The more frequently they explored, the more detailed the maps became. The farther they explored, the more broad. Likewise, as the migrations of seasons and stars were followed, temporal maps came into focus with greater acuity. Primate started to recognize patterns, in similarities and distinctions, of here and there as well as now and then.

Memories, associations, and patterns, later known as *knowledge*, layered invisibly within. As gradients of emotions were more easily distinguished, preferences were refined and associated with multiple possibilities. Based on past experience, good decisions could be made. Primate was learning. Unbeknownst to them, they were also learning how to learn.

At the time, learning was short-lived. The soft tissue of mental maps has a tendency to degrade. Many memories made in a lifetime were simply forgotten, abandoned to the mist. Memories which reached the finish line died quietly at expiration. Without symbols to document, knowledge was preserved in only one way: It was conveyed from one generation to the next through acts and observation.

Children acquired learning by observation and imitation of the acts of elders, neighbors, siblings, and kin; just as generations before had done. If, however, one did not act, or another did not observe, and repeat, all which curiosity had explored and confidence gained perished in a heartbeat. Knowledge, like a garden, had to be cultivated, culled, and practiced to be preserved.

With such short frames of reference, change was indistinguishable from continuity. Nothing seemed impermanent. Ignorance does not distinguish similarity from difference. Only experiences which were repeated, season after season, generation to generation, would bind to heredity's cellular information. Also, acute events of tremendous pain, or great love whisked suddenly away, adhered so tightly as to seem woven into the marrow.

Such memories felt so natural, internalized, and habitual as to seem unalterable, concrete, and real. These memories, and the feelings attached to them, were difficult to shake and settle. Only through efforts to (un)learn, along with a repetition of new patterns, within the spirit-mind and physically expressed, by one or all around, would the intensity of these felt-memories slip and fade. Without fluency, symbols, or documents, the details of a historical experience might be lost in a generation. The detachment of feelings from the memories, however, was a healing of the spirit-mind. Later the experience was given the name *forgiveness*.

As observations and experience expanded, Primate began to notice they had limitations. Tasks others could carry out were not within their abilities. Primates looked to neighbors to teach. The best teachers were those quite unlike themselves. Mimicry mixed with innovation taught Primate new ways to overcome their limitations.

For instance, Primate acquired considerable knowledge from their neighbors with wings. On occasion, they observed birds use their beak and a hard surface to crack open seeds. Alas, Primate had no beak and their fingers were much too large. Fingertips would receive the shock; the seed, left untouched. Whereas hunger mixed with anger choked creative thought, from hope and curiosity tinged with disappointment, inspiration erupts.

Primate sought new methods to accomplish similar tasks. In a reversal of strategy, Primate's fingers held a small rock like the beak holds a seed. Upon a flat stone, a small nut was held in place by the gentle hand of gravity. With one tap, the nutritious kernel was released from its shell of rigidity.

Primate witnessed crows use sticks to probe for edible insects. Primate plucked reeds, stripped them of their leaves, and pulled termites from their nests. Stout limbs were fashioned to locate the bees' hidden treasure. One end they frayed to extract honey from the hive, leaving it intact for next time. The neighbors' homes Primate admired as they ambled by. Nests and shelters of sticks, leaves, and tufts of fur kept neighbors warm and dry. Primate blended similar materials of larger size for safe shelters to sleep inside.

They watched turtles bask on branches and fish drift effortlessly downstream. A blade of stone they used to carve out a fallen tree and floated on a raft. The tree's limbs served as pikes to propel, steer, and, more importantly, to halt. No longer limited to four legs or to dry land, Primate explored spaces, and broadened maps, farther and farther from shore.

One morning, with the raft tethered to a tree, Primate dawdled on the banks of a winding river. Current drifted around ankles dangling in the water. Primate ate the sun in handfuls of fruit, nuts, and honey. Light glistened and danced in the flickering shade. A breeze stirred the leaves to decorous applause.

A lone bird sang. Then, an echo, a refrain. Two took turns in mimicry.

While Primate listened, the phrases branched and differed. Inflections fluctuated. So too the cadences. If a melody resolved on a lilting note, a threshold opened wide. The next phrase followed suit. Was that a call? Then, a reply?

With curiosity and attention piqued, Primate noticed patterns in the variety. Not only was there a call and response. Select sounds were offered up in certain situations, at certain times of day. At sunrise, for example, a song of celebration was thrust upward to the sky. In contrast, if a clutch of seed was found, a more secretive message was slung closer to the ground.

In times of imminent danger, an urgent message was spread. Though the sentinel divulged their location, the first to sense a looming threat was obliged to sound the alarm. With mindful attention, Primate noticed, the warnings differed as well. Before a storm arrived, less cautionary notes were cast into the wind. A new awareness within Primates' spirit-mind became vividly apparent. Whereas the youthful Primate had learned food was to be shared, their elders also knew to share truthful information.

Primate as well was able to generate a variety of sounds. Grunts spontaneously huffed when something heavy was lifted up. Groans oozed when sadness swelled. Deep sighs came as bliss swept in. Like the birds, Primate paired with a friend and began to organize the sounds.

An object, such as a stick or a seed, was grasped and extended as if to say, "This." A sound was vocalized. Then repeated. To their partner, a message was conveyed: "From now on, this particular utterance represents all objects like this one." Mental maps of memory and mutual agreements allowed simple sounds to represent objects remembered but unseen.

Anything within reach acquired a sonic symbol. Primate soon realized fingers could point to objects beyond arms' reach or to those too large to hold. A finger could point at the moon, for example. A sound was made. Yet Primate understood, the symbol was *not* the moon.

Sounds were associated not only with physical objects far overhead or those close at hand. They also symbolized actions witnessed by two or more. Sounds were sculpted first for objects as visible as nouns, then for events as fleeting as verbs. Sounds became symbols to re-present the seemingly permanent as well as the short-lived.

Sounds could also convey sensations unseen, but fully experienced. If an external event or object elicited an inner response, and if the feelings within could be understood by a neighbor or friend, a sound could be ascribed. Vocal symbols came to represent nearly everything meaningful to Primates; what happened around and within as well as the perspective of the participants.

The sonic symbols became useful tools. They could communicate the question, "Do you remember what happened?" as well as its response. In addition, if past patterns were recognized, future predictions could be expressed as well as contingent hopes. Conjectures could be brought forth. "Based on experience, this might happen next."

In times past, what had once been unspeakable would silently slip into the abyss of non-memory. Now, Primate could pass along that which had been observed, experienced, and learned. Sounds could represent the bees, their daily departures in search of flowers, and the delight in returning to a home intact. Sounds could represent the biting insect, its escape from the swat of a hand, and the desire to preserve life. Eventually, as a mirror might reflect upon itself, a sound was assigned to symbolize the symbol. The first assigned was *word. Names* soon followed. Words and names were inauspicious discoveries. Embedded in this seemingly benign tool, the disunity of division and separation had unwittingly begun. The misfortune was not to be the last. Nearby, yet another branch of separation was about to ignite.

In hindsight, no one quite recalled which actually came first. Audible sounds leave less of an impression than ashes in dust. In the units of time of the universe, it could be said that symbolic language arose concurrent with Fire's domestication. Like the elders, neighbors, siblings, and kin, Primate had long witnessed Fire scorch the land. Generally during the stormy seasons of light and heat, after a flash of lightening came crashing in, the land ignited in a wild, rambunctious burn. Until a soaking rain, the rampage was unquenchable.

While Fire blazed, neighbors rooted to the soil stood stalwart. Their migrations moved so slowly, Fire's rapid advance was unavoidable. The Rooted Ones could only hope Wind might shove Fire in another direction. Or that Rain might come from nowhere to quench the suffocating thirst. Otherwise, sheltered as seeds beneath the soil, the offspring of the Rooted Ones were the last remaining hope. A next generation may yet survive to replace the old growth and overstory after the elders were burned alive. Other neighbors on landlocked legs scurried hurriedly away. Primate, on the other hand, curious and confident, stood at a safe distance to observe what might happen next.

Fire followed a trail where the dry tinder lay to feed it. If Fire reached the banks of a wet stream, its advance abruptly ceased. With deep water just ahead, and the rear supply lines exhausted, Fire acquiesced. It could do little more than smolder while awaiting expiration.

As it lay dying, Primate cautiously approached. With careful observation, they noticed Fire could be tenderly restored to vibrancy. More importantly, Fire could just as easily be squelched. Someone among the clan of Primates, those with the unusual gait, assembled a set of disparate thoughts. Whereupon came a profound revelation.

With a tuft of grass, Fire could be rekindled. A stick could lift it from the ground. Upon two cautious feet, with two free hands, Fire could be carried aloft. Where it was laid, Fire could be nurtured and contained. Kept in its rightful place, Fire became a helpful ally to protect Primate in spirit and body.

In the cycles of darkness, Fire gave light. In seasons of cold, Fire lent warmth. To the community, Fire offered a point to gather around. Attention centered while meals were shared and information traded. In the exchange, Primate learned that the soft tissue of physical bodies stored energy from the sun and nutrients from the soil. In the rare seasons when the fruit of the vine was very sparse, Fire rendered intruders quite edible. Fire was assigned the responsibility to prime meat for digestion and metabolism.

The Primates with an unusual gait were now able to consume the sun's energy in three different ways. The first through eating the fruit of the vine. The second by burning the brush. And the third, in times of crisis, eating meat which was cooked. As they consumed more and more energy of the sun, Primate's manner of thinking changed. Those with the unusual gait so thoroughly differentiated themselves, their offspring gave them a new name: *Homo erectus.*

In the earliest increments on the unnamed planet, as the processes of Life and Love converged, the single-celled forebears harnessed the energy of the sun. A new equilibrium was launched. For well over ninety-nine units of time, the equilibrium had been well-maintained on one form of solar energy alone.

When Erectus domesticated Fire, however, one branch sprouted onto a separate equilibrium. From the peaceful center, they diverged. At first the new ability seemed indubitably brilliant. Only later did problems emerge. So beholden to Fire as they were, the offspring of late became the domesticated ones.

In the interim, Life and Love held firm with patient acceptance to evaluate the change. Could Fire be integrated and homeostasis maintained? If not, would Erectus' offspring halt and return? If the answers were in the negative, sadly, the new branch would be gradually, inexorably pruned.

> *Humility is knowing oneself as integral to a larger whole, a shimmering thread in a great web. When I fully grasp that I am part of all that is, part of life, part of the mystery, walls of separation break down. . . . I feel whole and complete; I am part of the dance of life and God, and I know that my soul has its particular role, which no other soul can fill. I feel my true nature as a sacred being in a sacred universe; I recognize that you too are sacred. This recognition leads me to ask: What is your story? What is your soul's journey about?*

The Path of Blessing: Experiencing the Energy and Abundance of the Divine by Rabbi Marcia Prager. (Jewish Lights Publishing, 2003, p. 46)

Harvesters of Sun

ooooo

We have come to the beginning of the final day of the ninety-ninth increment of time. Pause for a moment and notice: What arises within you at its mention? Excitement for a new beginning? Anticipation of the centennial ahead? Or fear and dread of an imminent finality? What do the feelings reflect about the predictions made? What do the predictions reflect about the maps in the mind?

Trust in this assurance: All is well. No need to worry. We are still far from the lived experience of our final destination. While you read these words, you are here, you are safe, you are loved. This too is a fundamental principle echoing throughout the universe. A day to the universe is not like one to us; nor are the notions of finality, fear, or dread. Indeed, as we will soon see, steadfast continuity flows easily even in the change to fractional units of minutes, or hours, or days.

Early in the final week of the final month of this ninety-ninth increment, our oldest parent, those Primates with an unusual gait, became numerous enough and distinct enough to be separated from their kin. Yesterday, *Homo erectus* died. As a harbinger of their off-spring's resiliency, the brevity of Erectus' life could be easily overlooked. No single event does a pattern make.

However, if the outcomes of our closest relatives were taken as a whole, there is ample reason to be more gravely concerned. None have lived long. In fact, only one still lives today. Our youngest parent, *Homo sapiens*, emerged a few hours after midnight on this the very last day. Orphaned in infancy, Sapiens were late to notice that no one like them remained.

As all Beings before, from the original seed to Cyano to Sapiens, emergence was followed by rest. Sapiens' Sabbath, like their age, was terribly brief and quick. In the late afternoon, as the sun began its descent, their Sabbath followed suit. The hours of accomplishment since have been a true astonishment. Breath-taking, mind-boggling, jaw-dropping, to say the least. Infancy to adolescence to adulthood careened at a breakneck pace.

During the Sabbath, Sapiens roamed far and wide. They soon came to realize that the unnamed planet, like their bodies, was mostly aquatic. Several expansive land masses were tenuously joined by bridges just beneath the coursing seas. When the moon was hidden, as the seas slept, a single star could guide them. In small boats, Sapiens crossed over. Land provided sanctuaries of refuge, but as in all such spaces, there were no guarantees.

Upon the great islands, Sapiens noticed, numerous Beings shared this home. Some had two legs. Some had four. Some had no legs at all. Those constrained to the land lived within a three-dimensional space. In two dimensions, bound by gravity, they moved from horizon to horizon on a level plane. In the third: upon a planet spinning through space. They meandered foraging for food, places to rest, and others with whom to play. If their neighbors took note of Sapiens, they were pleasant and friendly. Most, however, seemed too occupied with caring for each other to spare Sapiens any attention.

Sapiens noticed other, more magnificent neighbors had a much greater range. These could move in all directions within a four-dimensional space. Like their time-bound, landlocked neighbors, they could move between the horizons upon the spinning planet. Furthermore, with wings they elevated far into the skies. With fins, they could descend deep into the seas. They traveled in the six directions essentially as they pleased. Greatly enhanced were their abilities to seek food, safe shelter, and delight in expressive play. Poor Sapiens could only stare in awe at their flights of fancy.

Though Sapiens had no numbers, as of yet, with which to count, their neighbors hidden by the seas and sheltered among the trees far outnumbered them. If this aquatic planet with its enormous skies and islands of land belonged to anyone, certainly it was to those more numerous than Sapiens.

Like a visiting stranger, it seemed Sapiens had been extended a solemn invitation. If accepted, they could share in this space, this sliver in time, with their elders, neighbors, siblings, and kin. If Sapiens cared for the land, air, and water as if it were home, their presence would be welcomed. If they chose otherwise, as to where they may go, finding out would come the hard way. Outcomes remain undisclosed. Branches pruned are cast deep into an abyss of non-memory.

Upon the land, there was one with neither wings, nor fins, nor legs who impressed Sapiens more than all others. Humbly rooted to the soil, less perceptive observers might overlook this elder's great importance. They weathered stormy winds with strength and flexibility. Joined root to root, they firmly anchored each other to the soil. The underground matrix wordlessly conveyed information crucial to their health. Joined from branch to root by rippled bark, precious rain was channeled downward. Then from root to branch, nutrified water flowed up through inner capillaries. Year after year, green leaves unfurled to gather the sun's energy. With little assistance, they prospered through acts of generosity and simplicity.

The Rooted Ones were so efficient in their work, a surplus was freely shared. The Beings who stayed close to the land were very well-fed. Those who moved aloft found shelter, safety, and rest. Shade was spread as a respite for every passerby. With subtle respirations, they cleansed the atmosphere. Throughout the year, their leaves, stems, roots, and seeds provided medicine for ailing neighbors. In moments of spontaneity, beneath the illuminating sun, or the mysterious moon, leaves shimmied as bodies swayed. With Wind, they danced and played.

It seemed to Sapiens that every Being—those with roots, fins, and wings, on two legs and on four, and with no legs at all—all had a purpose to fulfill. Even Death and its sidekick, Decay. In the sequence of events, they performed their roles like naturals. At times, Death appeared suddenly. Storms still descended upon the planet with incredible force. At other times, a passerby may unknowingly trespass and transition into new-found prey. The material and energy of life could be instantly washed away.

Alas, if Sapiens intruded upon the space of a neighbor—their approach too quick, too close, or both simultaneously—a hard lesson was learned. Like a tuning fork, the memory reverberated to the third and fourth generations. Everyone was free to move and to occupy their own space. No one was needlessly killed nor permanently displaced.

Occasionally, Death came more slowly. Illness and injury were experienced universally. Illness might inhabit vulnerable bodies and the animating energy gradually fade. At times, within the arc of a single day. At others, Death's approach—when rain was sparse or winter bitter—could be spied from a season away.

Suffering, however, was completely unknown. Likewise, betrayal and abandonment. Not a mere coincidence. Hardships were never endured alone. To the elders, neighbors, siblings, and kin, Sapiens among them, the cycle of death, birth, and life was a sacred process. On occasions when one's vitality steadily faded, and friends came to love them at the bedside, the transition was gratefully accepted as a blessing undisguised. Life and Love was ever present. Long exhalations only succumbed to yet another deep inhale.

When Neanderthalensis, the last of our parents' siblings, suddenly reached the end of their brief life, they gave to our youngest parent, Sapiens, an astounding skill and gift. The elder taught the younger how to draw. The contribution to memory and abstract thought has ramified profoundly ever since.

With the development of vocal language, Erectus had learned to represent objects and events symbolically. When combined with the gift of visual drawing, their offspring learned how to record and preserve memories of experience. Knowledge could now be transmitted extrinsically across the space of villages and the time of generations.

Exemplary demonstration was no longer the sole method by which to teach. Nor observation, to learn. Knowledge converted into images of experiences, ideas, and beliefs could be preserved and passed along. If later generations retained a literacy of attention and interpretation, wisdom need not be suddenly lost nor fade away. From that day onward, generations could find a way home if corrupted ancestors strayed.

Once Sapiens understood the value of sharing truthful information, there came the time for sound education. Elders and children, teachers and students, encircled the communal fire. In the exchange, students as questioners led. They described the day's experiences of confusion and surprise, internal sensations they could now notice, distinguish, and identify.

The questioners sensed within them that a prediction had been made. Yet, somehow, expectations turned out differently. They wondered, "How or why did it occur in this particular way?" Their curiosity kindled, a field opened wide for stationary explorations of space, memory, spirit, and mind.

Then teachers took their turn, for neither did they know. More questions were forthcoming. They too must learn. To comprehend what had happened, the context must be thoroughly described. What did the questioners observe? What did they see, hear, smell, taste, and feel? Inside and out? The skin, gut, heart, and face were all sources of valuable information as were the eyes, ears, nose, and tongue.

Teachers listened closely. Then a final set of questions, "What had happened just before? What earlier events had formed their predictions, the pattern of memories from which today's events diverged?" Then, in closing, the teachers would ask, "What did you believe would happen next?"

Everyone listening understood. Nothing of the future could be known. Only imagined in hopes that it might appear in familiar robes. Automatic predictions were based on beliefs and patterns of past events, if any such patterns had been previously experienced. Beliefs were little more than ephemeral thoughts generated within the nascent mind. The more rigid the prediction or belief, the greater the surprise.

Indeed, knowledge, whether memory or imagination, is forever incomplete. Certainty is but a cunning deception, belief a clever ploy around which perceptions accrete. Tangentially related, one would hope, to a physical reality actually experienced, but such is never guaranteed. In any event, comprehension of past and present, like predictions of the future, is inherently limited.

As shadow and light flickered, the teachers paused, first to listen, then to breathe. The full context must be absorbed including the perspective of each participant. Before a word of wisdom could be offered, the aperture of heart and mind patiently softens, then dilates to full openness.

Whereas the students described *what* had happened, it was left to teachers to attempt an explanation as to *how* or *why*. When done well, subjective explanations could shade in the opaque space between memory and predictions, between uncertainty and surprise. Each novel and dissonant experience contributed to an emergent pattern. The mosaic of broken pieces was enfolded in a larger whole. Within degrees of uncertainty, the next piece might be reasonably predicted, but the future was interminably undetermined. In other words, whereas the past is partially comprehensible, the future is completely unknown.

This is what the teachers taught, what the students were meant to learn. Patient discovery leads to understanding. When taken as a whole, consonance can reconcile dissonance—if both are allowed to enter the open aperture of one's heart and mind.

Attempts at subjective explanations fell solely to the teachers but for one reason alone. On one hand, it was true, the creation of the minds of the teachers had been in process for an equally long period of time—equal with all elders, neighbors, siblings, and kin, including Sapiens. On the other hand, teachers held a slight advantage over questioners. From the sunrise of their birth to this most recent minute, within the flow of the web of Life and Love, they had been exquisitely attentive witnesses. Therefore, the mental maps they carried were generally more broad, more detailed in particularity, and oftentimes both simultaneously. The advantages brought awareness, later called *humility*: Knowledge was a process, emergent and forever incomplete.

The roles of teachers and questioners alternated in a seamless ebb and flow. Teachers continued to experience curiosity, perplexed confusion, and bright-eyed surprise. They too were students for life. The questioners' slight disadvantage, however, could never be completely overcome. Thus it was the teachers' responsibility to emulate wisdom, humility, empathy, and compassion with demonstrations that words were hamstrung to convey. With open hearts and open minds, they were rarely angry or shocked, alert but never afraid. To the best of their ability, they cared well for others during work, rest, laughter, and play.

When the campfire had smoldered into a warm, soft glow, the teachers and questioners slept. The planet's shadow cast a darkness over the land for a spell of nightly peacefulness. Then, as had happened for as long as Sapiens could recall, once more the sun arose. As birds sang their ode to the morning, a host of elders, neighbors, siblings, and kin were likewise beckoned to arise. A new day of effortless work—to flow, to teach, to care—had arrived. Afterwards, like clockwork, came the time to play. Each day's routine was regularly the same. A stable, predictable frame offered the widest range for creative acts of love and beauty—once again, a paradox.

In preparation for the tasks of the day ahead, Elders gathered the children to bring along. Those too small to walk were carried aloft. From their perch, like a lantern or lighthouse, they could observe. With eyes and ears like sponges, everything was absorbed. Nothing was overlooked. Neither a tittle nor a yod, not one iota was tossed.

Though far too young to translate memories into symbolic language, children retained each drop seen, felt, and experienced. Interactions between the elders were overheard. Sequences of tasks observed. Particular outcomes, purposes achieved, without a word came to be easily understood. If simultaneously an inner emotion was evoked, such as joy, shame, sadness, or fear, even longer did the new memory adhere, for better or for worse, that is.

With children astride, the parents roamed. To satisfy their metabolic need for the sun, the fruit of the vine was gathered. To satisfy Fire's ravenous hunger, cords of dried wood were stacked. For the ill and injured sheltered at home, fingers gingerly collected medicinal leaves, stems, and roots. Small amounts were taken. Much more, for later, was left in place.

Information too was gathered from neighbors. Equal in importance to food, wood, and medicine, truthful information aided preparations for the cycles known as the future, next season, and tomorrow. Along the way, Sapiens might also find soft materials to protect fragile but resilient bodies in motion. Coarse materials as well for the shelters where Sapiens slept and the places where the tools were kept. Once assembled, materials coarse and soft protected the flesh, and the Beings inside, from excessive sun, wind, cold, and rain, as well as the objects which supported life.

During these expeditions, no child was left behind. Parents were not separated from their children. From sunrise to sunrise, the care and education of children was always first and foremost in Sapiens' mind. Even before short legs stood them upright, children were carried along to watch and to learn.

In the earliest seasons, before the children developed a capacity to assess safety, risk, and sound decisions, they were always kept close by. At first within arms' reach. Later, within reach of the eyes. As the children's maps broadened, and new perspectives were sought, children could venture beyond the parents' sight, but stayed always within earshot.

As their legs gained in strength and coordination, children explored independently. From varied perspectives, new skills were learned. As their arms, hands, and fingers became more nimble, children were asked to assist. The elders' work was practiced firsthand. Sequences were enacted. Adequate force applied. A subtlety of touch came of age in fingers, spirit, and mind.

When released from the parents' full attention, children sought opportunities to craft mental maps of their own. Far could they roam, but they did not stray. They had no reason to hide or to lie. A return to safety was always easy to find. In the mind's eye, patterns converged. Children gained in curiosity and took small risks. Their confidence multiplied.

At the beginning of the final hour of the final day of the ninety-ninth increment of time, as with the domestication of Fire, another second-order change occurred. While Sapiens roamed to find morsels of food, they made a fascinating observation. When overripe fruit released from the vine, it fell to impregnate the soil. Later, in the very same spot, a miniature replica of the robust parent emerged. In due time, the little ones matured and bore fruit of their own.

Due to consistent consumption of the sun's energy, from the fruit of the vine and the burning of the brush, Sapiens was enabled to conceive of yet another new idea. In handfuls they gathered seeds from overripe fruit. Like wind, they carried the seeds closer to home. Like gravity, they delicately laid them in rows. Then they gently covered them with soil. As the tender sprouts emerged, Sapiens drizzled water around the tiny stalk and nurtured them as if they were one of their own. Later in the season, following Life and Love's Instructions, the plentiful attention was returned. The sprouts yielded fruit for all to share and consume.

Figs, the most delectable of fruits, were the first agricultural experiment. Sapiens patiently cared for the young sprouts. Before bearing fruit, young fig trees made three, four, then five trips around the sun. Patience was worthwhile. When the time was ripe, figs were a delicacy to behold. Sapiens also understood, much to their chagrin, that for healthy muscles, teeth, and bones, such succulence would not suffice. Thus, they planted hearty grasses, like barley and rye, for the abundant grains of seed as well as more versatile fruits of pistachio and olive trees.

By experimentation, Sapiens learned and practiced the art of agriculture. When neighbors who gathered the sun were well cared for and nurtured, energy stored could be harvested and shared. Energy, care, and good health endlessly cycled from plant to body to plant. Longevity found its optimum with consistent reciprocity.

With the newfound ability to domesticate the sun, less time was spent searching and gathering. More was freed for play and creativity. Imagination conjured up a cornucopia of ideas. Sapiens suddenly became more literate in the language of the universe. Consciousness expanded. Later consciousness gave itself a name, *Spirit*. Then came a nickname, more intimate and familiar: *Intuition*.

As a result, new medicines in leaves, stems, and roots were discovered. Tools of all varieties improved.

Shelters and structures were redesigned and built of sturdier materials. Seasons gave fewer reasons for anxious migrations en masse. No one went hungry. No one grew cold. The ill were more often cured. Those who were not did not die alone. Sapiens lived long as did their neighbors. In numbers, their villages grew.

After the advent of agriculture, and the expansive growth in population, a significant problem arose. If Sapiens continued to work in the traditional ways, the needs of the community could not be sustained. Sapiens could no longer work in large groups to perform one task at a time. Generalists heretofore, Sapiens had to begin to divide their labor and specialize in unique roles. Smaller groups would now perform tasks sequentially so multiple families could be served simultaneously. Each person within the small groups would be trusted to fulfill their niche responsibly. As is so often the case, with greater specialization came ever more interdependence.

A systematic method would be necessary to organize and coordinate these specialties of care. A bivocational role was devised to help guide the emergent system. The new role was given a title: steward-manager. While steward-managers continued to work within the small groups to serve their neighbors directly, time was allotted to consider new types of decisions. Steward-managers were the integument between the community of elders, neighbors, siblings, and kin, including Sapiens. They addressed any disharmony between the interdependent Beings—equal in all ways, but in relationship, one step removed.

The steward-managers were selected because they had the foresight to perceive a budding phenomenon. Long before the category known as "prisoner" was invented, they were aware of the "prisoner's dilemma." Two Beings, separated and unable to communicate, occasionally must make decisions which affect the outcomes of each.

Lacking prior knowledge or communicated coordination, each individual was likely to default to choices which brought them the most benefit, the least harm, or both. In such situations, the anonymous other should fend for themselves, or so the thinking went. Outcomes, as one can easily guess, were consistently less than optimal. However, if decisions could be coordinated, interdependent Beings would benefit more and lose less.

Therefore, *before* difficult decisions with incomplete information had to be made, participants learned the ways to act for the common good. Instructed in the needs of community, they mutually agreed to methods which generated the greatest benefit and the least harm for everyone. Cooperation was favored over competition, reciprocity over self-interest.

Since the Instructions were widely known and agreed upon, direct communication to coordinate care was rarely necessary. Third-party interventions as well. The steward-managers grew bored. Synchronous acts of care were more often coordinated silently by the

Instructions resonating throughout the web of Life and Love. In the verbose future, such coordination would be ascribed the names of *trust* and *unity*.

In extraordinary situations, lacking good communication, and prior agreements, as mentioned above, individuals might devolve to rely on narrow self-interest. The results, again, were less than optimal. As results rippled outward, the community as a whole suffered through the unfolding losses. Therefore, as these situations arose, a trustworthy intermediary was quite helpful. This was the narrowly defined, part-time role of the steward-manager: to assist with caring, cooperative interactions of those in extraordinary situations who could not directly communicate. And so it was that governance emerged.

Steward-managers and Sapiens realized that good governance was more art than science. Guided by principle and process, rarely for a particular outcome, the coordination of care was relational. Those skilled in good governance acted with humility to mimic the processes of Life and Love. They kept a wide perspective of the needs of the air, soil, and water as well as the elders, neighbors, siblings, and kin interdependent upon each other. The consenting community agreed to abide by the steward-managers' minimal decisions—to yield to a wider perspective opened by the states of mind later called *kindness* and *reciprocity*.

To respond creatively to the unpredictable complexities of life, good governance maintained simplicity. Thus, it was constituted of a mere three categories of rules. The first, that which was required, and the second, that which was forbidden, were stated explicitly. Everything else, left unsaid, was implicitly permitted.

A small number of acts were required of everyone. These acts to care for elders, neighbors, siblings, and kin elicited fundamental forms of Beneficence. If not consistently performed, the security of predictability, for the purpose of creative exploration, and the perpetuation of the multicellular community would unravel. To state this more succinctly, without Beneficence, continuity in the midst of change disintegrates towards disorder.

The second category, even smaller than the first, was comprised of the forbidden acts of Maleficence. Such acts were intuitively known to be harmful. If enacted, illness, injury, or death were sure to follow. The list was short because the reigning presumption throughout the community was that each and every one wished to avoid causing harm. Unless deviations from the Instructions of Life and Love were repeated, an explicit list of forbidden acts seemed redundant and unnecessary.

The third category, by far the largest, comprised all acts permitted. Some options permitted were much better than others. These were generally preferred. However, some acts permitted were not, in and of themselves, considered "good." These were generally avoided. Freedom of choice, by definition, allowed for the widest range of the window of tolerance. Personal responsibility, mutual trust, and consideration of the common good allowed Sapiens to live well within the window—and would deprive later tyrannies of their all-consuming energy.

The flexibility of a wide range of permitted acts eased constraints to creatively, cooperatively address unpredictability. The range also made room for friendly competition. Two or more groups could experiment, within the ethical limits of homeostasis, and discover a multiplicity of new and better ways to flourish.

Compliance with acts explicitly required and forbidden was managed with minimal enforcement. With collective consent for the common good and widespread personal integrity, overseers were unnecessary. Use of force was never permitted. Fear of violence and humiliation, the preferred means of control and domination, were completely unheard of. Such practices were only later adopted during a brief era of severe systemic inefficiency.

At the time, however, first mistakes were largely accepted because, on occasion, good choices can be difficult to predict—even more so to implement. When a poor choice was realized, a correction was voluntarily attempted by the one who was mistaken. Acknowledgment, apology, reparations, and a commitment to better future decisions were among the norms of the community.

If commitments were not upheld, appropriate sanctions were determined by the community at large including those who struggled to conform. Sanctions served like a shepherd's rod and staff. Before a member of the community strayed from the fold, a firm belief in the sanction's equal application discouraged wayward decisions. However, if a poor decision was repeated, the sanction was unequivocal. For instance, if an act which was required was repeatedly ignored, the neglectful one was undoubtedly immersed in opportunities to observe and participate in its benefits.

On the other hand, if one persisted in acts which were forbidden, the abusive one was withdrawn from further opportunities to cause harm. During the period of their sequester, they were assisted in learning the ways of Beneficence. Time and materials were provided to repair the prior damage done. Once restored to a healthy baseline of peaceful contentment, the one sequestered was slowly released. A process of integration within the community was accomplished by demonstrations of generous care and self-restraint.

If a rule, either forbidden or required, was regularly violated by multiple Sapiens, the rule was first scrutinized rather than the violators. Such evaluation was meant to discover if the rule had reached its expiration. If a rule was no longer honored, was the act widely considered permissible? Had the rule become superfluous? If so, the rule was deleted from the explicit lists of acts required and forbidden. The window of tolerance widened.

For an act to move in the opposite direction—no longer implicitly permitted and so added to lists of required or forbidden—was a much steeper climb. The needs of the community, and the Beings of whom it was composed, were prioritized over onerous rules and the privileges and power they imparted. Good governance and its clearly delimited constitution were designed to preserve inclusion in the community, freedom of movement, an even distribution of labor, and the meeting of everyone's needs.

In spite of the best efforts of the steward-managers, due to specialized divisions in the distribution of labor, stresses did emerge. The synchronicity of trade fell out of rhythm. The farmer, for example, worked every day so neighbors had food adequate for a thousand meals to circumnavigate the sun. The carpenter, by contrast, in the same length of time could build only one home. Then the family who dwelt inside had no additional need for many cycles to come. The tailor worked but a few days on clothing which protected a body for a season. The healer was always at the ready, but when they would be needed was irregular and unpredictable.

As a result, barter was no longer equitable. As often as the farmer fed the carpenter, there was no need for a new home. The healer changed clothes more often than the tailor fell ill. The prescient steward-managers realized a new tool was soon to come: A symbolic placeholder to denote that one Being had served another, but the provider was not yet in need.

Furthermore, as specialization, distance, and density cast a wider shade of anonymity, a new method was also needed to communicate information wordlessly. Recipients in remote exchanges desired a means to express their appreciation. "Thank you for supplying these. I needed this instead of that. In the future, I hope you can do more of the same." Therefore, the steward-managers deployed a new tool called *money*. It served as a placeholder to smooth the asynchronicity of commercial trade. It was also a means to communicate gratitude to neighbors noticed yet unseen.

Money was a stunning innovation, previously unimagined. Sapiens was the first, and still the only, to use anything of its kind. The idea was so unique, there were no models to emulate. Out of thin air, instructions for its use had to be invented. The first instruction stated that to briefly hold money was permitted, but its accumulation was forbidden. Money functioned only while in motion. Once it stopped, someone, somewhere, went without.

Therefore, the first instruction implied the second. Everyone agreed to receive a minimum compensation for their efforts. A smaller amount was more easily passed along and less likely to accumulate. Chances were reduced that some specialties might acquire an excess which lingered uselessly while others were deprived.

The third instruction dovetailed nicely with the two above. Provision of care was not contingent upon the amount of money on hand. If a neighbor had a need, the provider was obliged to provide. As a matter of reciprocity, neighbors requested only the minimum. No one could be denied their needs for any reason— neither age, nor ability, nor poverty. Indeed, poverty, as a concept, was unimaginable. Wealth as well. Not a mere coincidence. May those with ears hear.

If an excess began to accumulate, expedient redistribution was required. Surpluses were voluntarily relinquished to the community at large or neighbors in need. Otherwise, future troubles were easily foreseen. As stated above, if money accumulated in one home, in another there was a dearth. Out of pity or compassion, the one with too much might lend to the one who had too little, but the lender would someday insist upon the money's return. To avoid conflicts, the borrower would then feel compelled to strive for an excess. Their present expenses would still have to be met, and, in addition, the unmet needs of yesterday.

A corrupted wisdom would therefore lead to an errant belief: To avoid similar situations in the future, every opportunity to hoard money should be seized. Such acts signaled a dire systemic inefficiency. It was akin to water held behind a leaky dam or a heavy snowpack in spring. In the downstream path of destruction? The entire community.

To avoid such a calamity, these simple instructions put specialties in labor and money to good use:

- In your service, care, and work, give to the best of your ability, neither more nor less.
- Refuse no one their needs for material, energy, information, or work.
- So as not to overburden neighbors, when seeking one's needs, limit yourself to a full and complete minimum.
- Allow money to flow. Do not clutch or cling and sow the seeds of its accumulation.

With conditions in the community mutually agreed, it should come as no surprise that money was a useful tool for quite a long time. Unfortunately, as you may have guessed, Sapiens' use of money became badly distorted. The corruption was experienced universally, but the consequences were dealt unevenly.

With this in mind, we cautiously approach Sapiens' very recent downfall.

In a stroke, Thoreau swept the modern world away for a new world infinitely deeper and wider. . . . "I know of no book that has so few readers. There is none so truly strange, and heretical, and unpopular . . . 'Seek first the kingdom of heaven'—'Lay not up for yourself treasures on earth.'

"Think of this, Yankees!," he mocks. "Let but one of these sentences be rightly read from any pulpit in the land, and there would not be left one stone of that meeting house upon another."

. . . Genius, to be heard, must not out-run its audience—but Thoreau had left his audience far behind. Yet his fundamental insight never wavered: "Your scheme must be the frame-work of the universe; all other schemes will soon be ruins."'

Henry David Thoreau: A Life by Laura Dassow Walls. (University of Chicago Press, 2017, pp. 271–272)

Creators of Myths

ooooo

We are late into the eleventh hour; the last of the ninety-ninth increment of time. The path before us is crooked and rough. Hold fast to Hope. Please, do not be afraid. Once our destination is within sight, the uneven ground will be leveled like a plain. Life and Love patiently, persistently, illuminates the Way.

Landmarks appear more familiar, yet home is still far from sight. Three days ago, in the fractional units used thus far, our oldest parent, Erectus, domesticated fire. On this, the third day hence, our youngest parent, Sapiens, honored their origins through rituals for the deceased. Not long thereafter, less than three hours ago, Sapiens' last relative, Neanderthalensis, was lowered in the grave.

Two hours on and the eleventh hour dawned. Within fifteen minutes of its commencement, Sapiens had learned to domesticate the sun. Seeds were planted. Sprouts nurtured. Sapiens and neighbors were all well-fed. Right away Sapiens began to specialize and divide their labor. Agriculture and new systems of work freed time for the burgeoning populations. In the expanding space between work and rest, play cultivated imagination. Creativity was enhanced. Likewise abstract thought and innovation.

One innovation was the concept of money. A simple coin to hold a place in time for the exchange of needs and to convey gratitude for their provision. Money began to circulate at the bottom of this, the eleventh hour.

Ten minutes later, now forty into the hour, and Sapiens coined yet another innovation. Old Neanderthalensis' drawings were refined into symbols, later called *letters*, to represent the previous symbols of vocalized sounds. Letters were assembled into words: Approximations of translations two degrees removed from one reality. Sapiens eagerly coupled words into sentences like train cars of teacups too small for their freight. The words runneth over with power and meaning. Only the irony was retained.

Captions of words were appended to young Sapiens' drawings. As they aged, the captions lengthened. Grammar synthesized. Images waned. Abstract stories emerged. Oral stories once told by the ancestors were frozen, perfected, confused, and forgotten.

Symbols called *numbers*, like letters, were drafted; abstract concepts to quantify objects, money, time, and space. A form of grammar called *math* was invented to represent, measure, and divide. Trade was tabulated. Gardens evenly sectioned. Maps imposed unsightly boundaries upon the land. Structures rose higher. Bridges arched and lengthened. Days were divided. Calendars synchronized.

In eight minutes more, three quarters through the eleventh hour, an oral story was preserved in symbols of written words. Creation myths were transcribed. Myths born of limited witness reduced a complex world into hard documents. They formulated Sapiens' subjective interpretations to alleviate a modicum of confusion between prediction, preference, and surprise.

In times past, Sapiens' humble understanding was derived solely from experience. Upon the mental maps, a hedge was penciled in. On one side, Wisdom; on the other, Mystery. Sapiens maintained comfort with ambiguity and uncertainty. With the advent of a vibrant Imagination, however, brought on by agriculture, divisions of labor, and extended play, Sapiens began to speculate about Mystery with abstract stories crafted in the mind. Somewhere along the way they leapt over Mystery's hedge. On one side remained the infinite intricacy of a unified reality. But now on the other was what some preferred to be true instead.

In millions of ways minuscule and stressful in the immediacy, as well as a handful chronically destructive, Sapiens' offspring attempted to define a false reality. Then they attempted to enact the stories crafted by the imagination. Many believed so fervently, the stories seemed factual. Most concerning of all, they lost the ability to distinguish the difference.

The myths were noble attempts to make sense of a novel situation. A mere seventeen minutes ago, four millennia in Earth-years, Sapiens' offspring suddenly found their lives had been upended. Some neighbors had devised selfish manipulations of the rules of money, work, and authority.

Voluminous power was accumulated, often violently, by a small number of Sapiens. Lesser degrees, labeled *privileges*, were widely distributed to bribe complicity. To mold the bricks and erect the pyramids, Pharaoh and his [*sic*] minions set forth to control the people.

As a result, two new concepts were coined to represent motivations and experiences. The first was *evil*; the second, *suffering*. Two notions never before conceived in the entirety of the universe. From these two, many more would spill forth, such as *enslavement* and *exploitation*.

First came Pharaoh. Then the Babylonians. Then the Romans occupied the seat at the head of the table, the first of a long dynasty of EuroAmericans. Though the site of centralized power may drift, the suffering of inequality holds firm.

Sapiens' offspring throughout the kingdom were locked in states of opposition. Many struggled to escape. Some made it out alive. Most preferred to submit and play their part. With rewards and penalties so great, decisions to submit were easily made. Privilege and power, rewards and penalties, do corrupt. Often surreptitiously.

Under the proper conditions, as Pharaoh well knew, like fire and plants, Sapiens could be domesticated too. The people enslaved, however, were imbued with an innate sense of freedom. Pharaoh never could cleanse them of this spiritual-energetic sense. Try, try as he might, of Hope and Freedom Sapiens could never be dispossessed.

Based on prevailing norms and conditions, however, options for escape seemed few and far between. For those distorted and corrupted by power, privilege, and wealth, exercising the freedom to choose equality was like a sacrifice of one's first born. The bait had been eaten. The hook was set. Fortunately, for those willing to harness the courage, and put forth the effort, Life and Love stood ready, with arms wide open, blind-folded, unconditionally awaiting their embrace.

Following the advent of evil and suffering, of inequality, power, and wealth, a new tool was needed to bind together interdependent Beings heaving against the strain. Listeners of a sacred melody quietly humming through the universe attempted to re-present the Instructions emanating from a tiny mustard seed. The universal ethic of care was reduced to words as a reminder of their origins, relationships, and equality.

The weaving of the new binding began unceremoniously. No money or materials were available. Tools which threatened Pharaoh were scarce. With the aperture of heart and mind opened wide, silent meditations and patient observations were sufficient to initiate the process. Later there would be the gatherings; free exchanges of literacy and ideas; and ultimately incessant demonstrations of care and reciprocity—a revelation, a reweaving, of the web of Life and Love.

Another day of labor on Pharaoh's pyramid was complete. Weary Sapiens gathered by the fire to rest and contemplate. Questions were openly asked. Teachers recalled the days of their youth when similar questions had been pondered. Yet, the freedom, the hope to speak them aloud had long been put asunder.

Questioners sensed something, or someone, Mysterious hovered around or within. There seemed to be something, somewhere, out there, in here, much larger than themselves. Whatever, whoever, It was, It is, I am. It exists. A felt-sense of firsthand experience confirmed within Sapiens' belly, heart, and mind: curiosity, compassion, and courage stirred an irrepressible drive. Questions were raised in hopes of deeper understanding:

"From where did we come?"
"Why are we here?"
"Where does the Spirit go,
if it goes elsewhere?"

Answers were elusive. Possibly they preceded memory, language, and abstract thought. To reduce potential responses into symbolic words seemed a daunting task. Nonetheless, with great humility, a valiant effort was put forth. Sapiens entrusted Intuition emanating from the Original Source. It too had been woven of the same threads as the tapestry of the universe.

The question of "Why are we here?"—oriented as it is towards the perpetual present—provided a natural starting point. Answers to questions of where Sapiens came from, and where they were going, were inextricably bound into why we are here. We were born to peacefully care for our elders, neighbors, siblings, and kin; to give to the best of our ability; to receive only as we need; to learn, adapt, and teach before the baton is passed, through our death, so Life and Love goes on for perpetuity. Anything more was commentary. Anything less, simply incomplete.

To accommodate the intensifying pace of work under Pharaoh's enslavement, and the diminishing spans of attention, stories told around the fire began with an opening act and Sapiens situated front and center. For similar reasons, the stories concluded in grand extravagance. The protagonists—all played by Sapiens, of course—were the incarnate cosmic hero and the imperiled subjects cowering in distress.

Such notions of the beginning and end were contrived to frame the narrative limits of attention and comprehension. They are intellectual prostheses to sum up human experience. With apparently nothing more meaningful before, during, or after, as the story was told, Sapiens' offspring came to hail themselves as the one and only actor of any importance.

As the stories propagated, elders, neighbors, siblings, and kin were relegated further and further into supporting roles, an allegorical cast of scapegoats, metaphors, and foils. To keep attention where it thinks it belongs, flattened characters were an accommodation to Sapiens' learned self-centeredness. It was for this reason that translations of the universal ethic of care, later called *religious thought*, spun so far out of control.

With Sapiens firmly established as the center of attention, the Director hovered offstage just behind the curtains. He [*sic*] played His part to pull the strings and work the lights. All the while the adoring Director preened for the lead. From backstage, He impatiently waited while His love went unrequited.

The Director was intimately aware of all things Sapiens: their mannerisms, their foibles, their health. Not a hair on the head went uncounted. In fact, He may have been more than a little obsessed. In the entire realm of the history of the universe, nothing distracted the Director from Sapiens and their behavior. With the characters stationed in their rightful places, and the drama well underway, the story proceeded naturally towards an apocalyptic end.

Sapiens, as the story was told, had been created slightly lower than the angels—and by implication, over and above everyone else. In one-on-one comparisons with all expressions of Life and Love, across the entire history of the entire universe, some offspring hailed themselves as the most advanced. In its creativity, the human imagination is absolutely unsurpassed. It can be the most easily persuaded, and curiously, the most difficult to correct.

Sapiens' offspring became so numerous, and so steeped in the inequality of privileges and suffering, disagreements were rampant. On the status of their superiority, however, nearly everyone agreed. Fortunately, a steadfast remnant held out. Hope, like Freedom, had a foothold and never would release.

If, in fact, the offspring of Sapiens had been among the Beings most advanced, they would also have been the safest, healthiest, and most content. Yet, if one gazes across the landscape of these last minutes of the eleventh hour, their lived experience seems far from such for ones so intelligent. Distrust and dissatisfaction are as rampant as the disagreements. Likewise, anger and fear. Neighbors face violent danger that in any other time or place would be impossible to comprehend. The happiest demonstrate a version of a game children once called "Pretend." On the newly named planet called *Earth*, something seems to have gone terribly awry. Perplexed yet hopeful elders, teachers, and children began to ask themselves:

"How did we get here?"
"From where did we diverge?"
More importantly, "What will
happen next?"

In light of the troubles, to address the perennial questions allow the aperture to narrow for a moment of closer inspection. A minority among them have occupied a supermajority of positions of authority at most levels of organized society. Strangely enough, this minority all share three traits in common. The correlations cannot be easily dismissed. The minority were grouped and divided as able-bodied, heterosexual, and male.

It is safe to assume most of this minority tried their level best. Unfortunately for everyone, including the minority, a corruption spread through the inherited scripts. Equally unfortunate, due to their overbearing dominance, generation after generation, very few points of comparison exist. Would other leaders with other scripts have yielded other results? For the better or, heaven forbid, worse?

Now, allow attention to focus even more closely. A subset of the minority grew to maturity upon one of the seven continents. They lauded themselves as the most deserving; those upon whom all focus should rightly attend. By their own proud admission, among all others, they were the most exceptional, the most dominant. In the colonization of lands, bodies, cultures, and beliefs, particularly in the areas of religion, science, economics, and language, they were unsurpassed.

As a group, none to date, not even Pharaoh, have been able to export their unwelcome violence and greed upon other parts of the planet like the men of European descent. This subset of the offspring were so distinguished they acquired a unique identity all to themselves. They became known as *EuroAmericans*. A term to concisely identify where they matured and how far they strayed.

As the aperture reopens, let it not be said that other members from other continents are therefore innocent; that is, those who managed to survive, or were left untouched, by EuroAmerican migrations and colonization. They may have troubles of their own with the distortions of gender, caste, privilege, power, and violence. But western civilization, to use a term liberally, widely disseminates a self-aggrandizing history of the victorious. Likely better known by you, the reader, and your guide, who is more prophet than historian at that, from here on out our attention focuses on the EuroAmericans.

Less than seven minutes ago, in the fractional units of the universe, the universal ethic of care was co-opted for ill intent. The edifice was preserved. The cornerstone, rejected. A method to bind us together, later called *religion*, was used instead to divide and to twist.

The Word, as written, so they said, was inspired by a Divine hand. It was perfect, inerrant, and interpretable only by men. Those ordained by a higher power, that is. Anyone who questioned their authority, or their infallible interpretations, was at first smugly ignored. If dissent persisted, the rhetoric heated up. Dissenters were disobedient, sinful, heretics, enemies of the state. The most incorrigible were condemned to die; to be mutilated, burned, hanged, or crucified.

In the beginning, as the story was told, a new word, *human*, was defined. Instantly, humans were granted dominion to name and to rule. They claimed *power*, a concept previously unheard of, over every living Being. Humans seized rights to colonize everything and everyone—despite the fact that no one else understood a word they said. From that day forward, Sapiens were no longer to consider themselves as equals with elders, neighbors, siblings, and kin. They were no longer at-One with the Web.

The notion of power infiltrated their spirits and minds. It knew no limits. It knew no ends. Even the

Ineffable was ascribed a name, a gender, and a place: just offstage and far overhead. The first division was rendered complete and it was deemed good.

In the second act of creation, the religious interpreters divided the humans on the basis of anatomy. Those with facial hair and penises were called *men*. Those without, *women*. Half went one way, half the other. Their rightful places clearly designated, the roles, behavior, and attitudes were easier to define: To the right, *masculine*; to the left, *feminine*.

According to the infallible interpreters, distinctions were to be strictly kept. Deviations were an abominable sin, a novel concept without precedent. The freedom to Be became unforgivable. With verdicts prejudged, a minimum sentence was declared: inescapable torment in a fiery abyss for eternity.

Before the sun had set, the horizontal separation of men and women, side by side, was stood on end. Men were above, women below. Men were associated with the head and shoulders: the source of all rationality, strength, and power. Women were associated with the heart and womb: deep wells of erotic desire and emotional instability. In the authoritative view of a particular minority, women were best seen, looked at, touched, and unheard.

On occasion, the imposed silence escaped its container. Resistance was expressed. Once put back in their place, however, women dutifully followed the commands of the rational head: Raise the children into obedient workers, stoic warriors, selfless nursemaids, and humble slaves. Then tend to the home, the gardens, the aging parents, and, last but certainly not least, service their leader, provider, and spouse—or any man who so desired.

Boys, on the other hand, were taught the ways of masculinity—strength, hard work, haughty inaction, and utter disregard. Anger, lust, and pride were permitted, respected, even encouraged. Sadness, regret, fear, and remorse were strictly forbidden. With no healthy practices of self-restraint, by early adulthood their violence, selfishness, and unapologetic greed overwhelmed the men and their neighbors equally.

By the age of full maturity, men were successfully sequestered into bifurcated states of stoicism and rage. The insidiousness of unchecked authority severely impaired their abilities for reciprocity, fidelity, and selfless care. Handcuffed by power, privileges, and the fear of losing both, their loneliness and isolation could never be admitted. The second division was thus complete, and it too was deemed good.

In the third act of creation, the EuroAmerican men noticed that not all humans fell in love in the same way. Some exercised the freedom to love those with bodies much like their own. They bonded naturally and cared for each other, often for life, with less emphasis on making babies or the religiously defined roles. It was as if some believed there was more to Life and Love than disseminating sperm and dominating a mate.

Such relationships the EuroAmerican heterosexual male simply could not tolerate. If humans were allowed a wide range of options and the freedom to choose, hierarchies, once erected, go limp. Homosexuality was thus forbidden; a sin never to be transgressed. Sex and sexuality were made taboo, never to be discussed, neither in the public sphere nor in the privacy of one's home. Taboos proved effective at stoking the ire of the hateful and stifling the shamed.

Thenceforth, men were commanded to marry only women, to wed with them for life. Such arrangements mitigated their stunted abilities to care for self, family, and neighbor. In addition, with one woman always at their disposal, the obsessive pursuit for sex may be alleviated, or at least moderated, to a degree.

On second thought, the command may have functioned in the reverse. Women may have been told to stand by their man for life. Regardless of the terror experienced, leaving was strictly forbidden. Divorce led to torment for eternity. In this world, however, transgressions were to be forgiven unconditionally, even if exceeding seven times seventy. With the freedom of movement thoroughly constrained, disparities were firmly entrenched. The third division was complete, and it too was deemed good.

In the fourth act, the EuroAmerican men basked in the sun alone upon the shore. Across the Mediterranean Sea they stared. Strangers, neighbors unfamiliar, were rowing towards the beach. Their skin was as dark as night. The EuroAmericans startled with fright and said, "Quickly, from them we must separate. Create a new division, *ex nihilo*! Let us call it *race*." They opened their Bibles immediately, to Genesis chapter nine, and in the pristine margins, scribbled the Curse of Ham.

From that day forward, the EuroAmerican men thought of themselves as *white*. Their neighbors from the south, *black*. In their self-imposed fear and ignorance, the dark-skinned neighbors were described as aggressive, lazy heathens. The EuroAmerican men thus established themselves as the standard bearers for all which was civilized, superior, and good.

Based on the inflated self-image, EuroAmericans were to be associated with the symbols of white and light. Others would perceive them as worthy and pure. All things dirty and evil, therefore, were associated with symbols black and dark. In hindsight, the choices were quite astonishing. The Bible they worshiped and adored often associated whiteness with lying and disease. Darkness was the source from which the Divine Light proceeds. Despite the incongruity, the fourth division was complete and, like those before, deemed good.

As the sun rose on the fifth act of the EuroAmericans' creation, men debated the question, "Who is my neighbor?" And thus, by inference, who was not. Faithful listeners scurried to define a new concept, *citizens*. Inside a government office, neighbors were separated and ranked by the proximity of their birth. If one was born nearby, north of the sea, and therefore white, like us, they were named citizens. Such well-defined neighbors were to be supported, cared for, and loved. Those born further away, and different in appearance, were dubbed *foreigners* and, often, *enemies*. Citizens were permitted to shun, exploit, brutalize, or kill, but rarely to love, the dark-skinned foreigner. One of many privileges of citizenship.

Privileges of citizenship were later renamed *rights*. With a subtle rebranding, bearers of privileges could have the best of both worlds. Rights were universal. All humans qualified. To the sub-human, rights were cleverly denied. In this way, the privileged beneficiaries of inequality preserved a feeling that they were inclusive, equal, and simultaneously a cut above. EuroAmericans were tacitly reminded, lest they lose sight of the reason why they, unlike others, were nominally free. They were the good guys [*sic*]. The implicit message was clearly received: "Stay obedient please. Otherwise, you too might lose your rights and privileges."

With the newly established designation, other concepts emerged. Places were known as *here* and *there*. One was *in*. The other, *out*. Neighbors, like us, belonged inside. Foreigners were kept out. Dark-skinned neighbors born further away, yet still free to move about, might occasionally sneak in. They found work, built homes, planted gardens, and sent their children to schools. At times the dark-skinned sons flirted with the light-skinned daughters.

Such behavior unnerved the citizens terribly. If the foreigners stayed much longer, they might come to think of themselves as equals. They would want to wed. Then there would be the children. If roots were established, EuroAmerican heritage, and inheritance, would be threatened; their exceptionalism obscured.

At first, the EuroAmericans politely encouraged the dark-skinned foreigners to leave voluntarily. A nudge of the elbow, a tilt of the head, the wink of the eye, all directed southward.

If the first request was not understood, unwanted neighbors were told, in no uncertain terms, the time had finally come. "Go back to where you were born!" If the warnings were ignored, foreigners could be forcibly removed, exiled, and deported. Once again, quite surprising since the Bible ostensibly worshiped by the EuroAmericans explicitly reminded them to be hospitable for they too had once been strangers in the land.

Furthermore, strangers who worshiped different gods, as well as neighbors who worshiped the same God in different ways, were punished similarly. If eviction to a distant land was prohibitively inconvenient, such strangers could be publicly lynched. In God's name, of course. The public hangings, the charred remains, clearly warned the witnesses: "Convert to the ways of the EuroAmerican. Be like us; not them. Spare yourself the test." To the third and fourth generations, the memories enmeshed. The fifth act seemed good indeed; or so thought the EuroAmericans.

As communities grew more homogeneous, those isolated inside felt segregated. (Or rather, disintegrated. Two linguistic symbols for one reality.) Detached from information and experience, false assumptions arose. Strangers were believed to be uncontrollable, unmanageable, and uncivilized. Differences and diversity elevated the fear and threatened the ignorance of the EuroAmericans. Campaigns for purity and the cleansing of ethnicity were so successful, EuroAmericans became morose. It seemed as if everyone were once again equal. No one felt special in the unfair competition of "us vs. them" with no "them" beneath their blood-stained feet.

For the penultimate act of creation, a less gruesome method was contrived to separate EuroAmericans from unwanted neighbors inside. A new concept, *crime*, gave rise to a new status, *criminals*. Crimes allowed trade and population to be regulated with less finality. When times were tight financially, unwanted neighbors born nearby, and the foreigners allowed in, could be kept and punished alive.

Catching criminals also gave EuroAmericans a new sport to relieve their anxious minds. If a criminal ran away, or approached too quickly, or remained still when told to move, or stood too aggressively, or spoke when told not to, against them lethal force could be used. Neighbors became target practice made live. Those fortunate enough to survive the arrest were imprisoned until times turned more prosperous.

Such separations were meant to be only temporary, of course. Prisoners were to submit and conform to the hierarchy of EuroAmerican, masculine ways. Imprisonment in crowded cells or solitary confinement were meant as mild forms of correction. Anything short of death to coerce a change in behavior. State-sponsored execution was reserved only for the most incorrigible. With criminals silenced and hidden away in plain sight, the ashamed in hushed tones could smugly say, "You see, we are not like them," and feel better about themselves.

The methods of mild correction were also enacted far beyond prison walls. Women and children in the home, like criminals behind bars, and foreigners in the field, took the brunt of EuroAmerican masculine violence. Insatiable EuroAmericans built great ships to export their hierarchy, greed, and violence to far and distant shores. The pioneers landed with great ferocity. Later waves rolled in with more sophisticated means to impose inequality and suffering.

The EuroAmerican men were down to their final act. No rest would they permit. Endeavors were short of perfection and time was running out. They had one last twist to foist upon their neighbors. If effective, it would endure for generations. In spite of the hierarchy, the creators of myths could easily foresee, so strong was the natural propensity for cooperation, a group of humans of differing genders, races, religions, and places of birth, yet of one heart and mind, might still come together to care for each other and flourish universally. This they could not tolerate. Something must be done. Their creation must never grow limp or die.

Therefore, a new interpretation was inscribed into the EuroAmerican religious narrative to be exported and imposed as far as they may roam. No longer would Jubilee be an event collectively experienced by everyone. No longer would their futures be bound together in peace for eternity. The people of the land must utterly forget the meaning of Shalom. Something called *salvation*, from here on out, would be doled out individually.

Prior to the days of Pharaoh, and the inequality of superiority and suffering, salvation as a concept was completely unheard of. Prior to the abuse and neglect of the poor, widows, orphans, and strangers the Bible itself was unnecessary. The universal ethic of care had no need to be transcribed. It was embedded in the processes of Life and Love, as Instructions of Matter and Energy, as seeds within a Seed.

Thus the jilted, off-stage Director was cast for a new role. In the midst of insufferable inequality, He [*sic*] would now play the part of Judge, Savior, and Redeemer. In the early stages, the character was jealous, vengeful, and mercurial. Miracles and punishments alike seemed capricious and inexplicable. In the second half, the role transfigured. A divine and gentle shepherd patiently pursued his lost and broken sheep. Then with mild persuasions, He tried to coax them back to follow in obedience.

As time progressed, salvation would be described with innumerable written and spoken words. It was to be a discretionary gift, offered individually, after death, in spite of the humans' innate, inherited, inescapable sin. Grace, unmerited love, forever undeserved, would be universally available—for those who commit, without questions, and willingly abide by the terms.

The Savior offered jndividual believers a bargain difficult to reject. With an outstretched arm, He pointed the way to a promise of life beyond death. At the very next stop, Paradise awaits. To achieve everlasting victory, the elect need only choose obedience to the all-male leaders—the powers and principalities, religious, commercial, and legislative—to their interpretations as well as their commands. The alternative, you ask? The fiery pits of Hell for eternity. Methinks I heard the Devil proclaim: "There was no coercion. No collusion. None whatsoever, I say!"

Throughout the interregnum, the living struggled daily. While less fortunate neighbors suffered, those of better fortunes supped their cold comfort like a delicacy. Little did anyone know, the trials and tribulations had only just begun. The creation of the social hierarchy was complete, but up ahead was no Sabbath nor perfect Paradise. A serpent lay in wait named *Economicus*.

So strong is this propensity of mankind to fall into mutual animosities, that where no substantial occasion presents itself, the most frivolous and fanciful distinctions have been sufficient to kindle their unfriendly passions, and excite their most violent conflicts. But the most common and durable source of factions has been the various and unequal distribution of property.

The Federalist Papers X, by James Madison, originally published 1787–1788. (Bantam Books, 1982, pp. 44.)

Overseers of a Pyramid

ooooo

Midnight is nearly upon us. The toll of the bells is only a few minutes away. Yet, at 256 revolutions per minute, there is still a fair distance to travel. Several hundred orbits will elapse prior to arrival. No need to tarry. Nor to rush. Patiently, persistently, onward we press.

With time and space framed so minutely, distinguishing transitions blurs. In such small fractions, beginnings and endings become more difficult to discern. Though the instability of change occurs incessantly, a perceived sense of powerlessness pervades. In spite of the frequency of decisions, immutable continuity seems to overpower. Contrary to outward appearances, opportunities for new trajectories emerge moment by moment and day by day.

Before the universal ethic of care was co-opted, the Instructions embedded in the tiny mustard seed conveyed an unspoken, unwritten message to all Beings upon the web of Life and Love. Everything had been freely given to be equally shared by all. Elders, neighbors, siblings, and kin gave to the best of their ability and took only as they needed. Land and water were commonly shared and from no one withheld. Unconditional exchange was managed by the Instructions bequeathed from our Greatest Great-Grandparent. Continuity in the midst of change regulated creative divergence, cooperative convergence, and contented equality. Homeostasis was perpetually maintained.

As EuroAmericans' self-serving interpretations of their Scriptures devolved, another of Sapiens' offspring, later known as *Homo economicus*, wished to add a few interpretations of their own. They surveyed the hierarchy as erected. It was indeed beautiful to behold: Quite slender, very tall. Although to eyes more critical, its stability teetered precariously. If ever it were to tip and fall, those on the upper rungs risked significant injury.

Economicus desired a more imposing shape. The society they envisioned was wide at the bottom and tapered as it rose. It would defy the universal law of gravity with a dynamism that drew wealth and power from bottom to top. An organization such as this would be difficult to topple while immense prosperity was suctioned up.

A solid foundation was stacked like bricks of all neighbors unlike Sapiens. Layered upon that very broad base was the vast majority of humans, grouped and divided as women, children, seniors, foreigners, and neighbors with disabilities or darker hues of skin. A plurality of EuroAmericans composed the middle layer. They were the pedestal upon whom the aforementioned minority reposed. From this middling position, they could also serve as tireless monitors of the underlings who slaved, then withered, below.

To execute such a plan, Economicus knew, would be quite a challenge. Odds were decidedly against. For so few to take from so many, the scheme must be extraordinarily diabolical. Success would require widespread complicity. The EuroAmerican male's contrived superiority must seem admirable when compared to the misery of everyone else. Only in such an environment would so many strive to be like them—those exclusively permitted, of course. The more miserable the Beings beneath, the more convincing the comparisons, and the more motivated the response. Resistance would be lowered. Compliance increased. Outcomes achieved. Voilà!

Mechanisms must also enable the material wealth of innumerable humans, through a lifetime of effort, and generation after generation, to be gradually siphoned off. A much smaller number would reap their loss. The sluice in between, the moderate middle, would contentedly hold the line. To achieve a tie as the impoverished failed would feel like victory, a sure sign that the system worked efficiently.

A handful, of course, would need to ascend to join the small group above. A narrow path of upward mobility to stoke the meager hopes of those less fortunate. A smattering would climb the steps to replace the losses due to erosion and attrition. (Addiction's costs were kept well hidden. *Externalities* became the preferred euphemism.) Economicus wished for a market where trade was anything but free. What they designed was a vast, adaptable pyramid scheme.

No one recalls who first conceived of such a dastardly plot. Based on outcomes, the name was likely not Eve. In point of fact, some evidence is indisputable. Whoever the culprit, they began with a belief previously unthinkable. More of the material and energy freely given to be equally shared was theirs to keep. They deserved it. Others did not. Whoever conceived such a belief, like Adam before them, has evaded responsibility. The name may be lost to ignominy, but to this very day the habit persists.

To be implemented, they must have had the help of a few close friends. Nothing meaningful can be accomplished alone. Change evolves in predictable patterns. Minor divergences precede broad adaptations. If hope, courage, and trust converge, fertile soil ripens for co-operative, interactive Beings to emerge. Without them working in tandem, however, the good fruit spoils.

Lacking better instincts, the secret club sought to satisfy their omnivorous appetites. They began to hoard that which was meant to move. Their bodies developed a gnawing hunger; even when stomachs were full. As a mission statement, they adopted a chant: "Takers keepers, losers weepers!" Unto death, they pledged to keep it sustainable. In this way, no one ever had to stomach the words, "Stop!" or "No!"

As the hoarding accumulated, more contented neighbors noticed a change. Inexplicably, fewer tokens of gratitude were circulating. The needs for housing, food, medicine, and protection had not decreased, nor had their ability to provide. And yet, trade had somehow declined. Some neighbors, lacking tokens but with a moral compass still intact, felt compelled to ask for even less. Others simply did without. EuroAmericans began to conceive of new categories. Among them were the *Have's* and the *Have-Not's*.

A new separation wedged in. A pernicious asymmetry grew. *Scarcity* became a word to symbolize the visceral experience of a few. All that was needed to flourish and thrive remained well within sight. Yet now, for some, it was kept slightly out of reach. The hoarding of money had raised the specter of Poverty; its inseparable, ill-begotten twin Wealth; and the insidiousness of Inequality.

Out of nowhere, fear emerged. Like water, it seeped into every crevice and every pore. Providers clutched what neighbors needed. Warily their fists released. Consumers grew restless. Someday might they be denied the means of their survival? Economic fear mixed with hierarchical divisions rose like a mounting flood. Together they evoked a new phenomenon, later known as *competition*.

Fear spread slowly, but steadily. Due to Economicus' secrecy and shame, the steward-managers were caught unawares. Suddenly, a new tool had to be devised: A psychological barricade to stop panicky humans from wildly taking that which remained within sight but was kept away from grasping hands.

The barricade could not be static, however. Materials could not be locked away forever. The dynamism of commerce, if sustained, must be well-regulated. If providers allowed a mechanism to release their goods and service, the withholding of their neighbors' needs could be physically enforced. Thus, in the name of balance and neutrality, Economicus and their Market were appeased. This was the steward-managers' first mistake, but far from their last.

Of course, implementation may have occurred in the reverse. Instead of anonymous consumers hoarding money, and instilling fear, providers may have been the first to opt out of caring for their neighbors. They may have unilaterally determined, regardless of the loss, some humans were simply undeserving, indeed less-than-human, worthless to keep alive. Those so unscrupulous were never memorialized. Nor has anyone, as of yet, claimed responsibility.

Motivations in this scenario would include fear and its corollary, hate, rather than unadulterated greed. If this were the case, the steward-managers legalized the withholding, but sought to appease impoverished customers by forcing the providers, against their will, to release the neighbors' needs. In either circumstance, outcomes were unchanged.

The unique innovation devised by the steward-managers was called *ownership*. A concept conceived exclusively within the figments of the human imagination. If the money on hand was insufficient to procure a release, owners were permitted to withhold from their neighbors anything they might need to survive. In addition, owners were assigned the power to dictate, like a ransom, the price of release. Any consequences, regardless of how tragic, were considered meaningless.

The concept of ownership was implemented slowly. Radical changes must start small. Humans need time to grow accustomed to new ways, after all. The steward-managers decreed that if there were options to acquire a lesser substitute, only the better of the two could be owned, withheld, bought, and sold. EuroAmericans had been primed to accept the divisions of better and worse. Some material objects, like their neighbors, were assumed to be more worthy than the rest.

As more people began to accept the new idea that some material objects and energetic work could be owned and withheld, valued, ransomed, and released, the concept spread. Everyone wished to be, and to own, what was valuable and superior to everyone else. Owning and withholding thus escalated the cost of release.

Eventually, the concept of ownership was applied almost universally. Only sunlight, gravity, and air managed to escape. Everything else under the sun, it seemed, could be owned and withheld. Indeed, the physical work to care for each other and to preserve life was ransomed. Neighbors were forcibly captured, auctioned to the highest bidder, and permanently named as *slaves*. Others surrendered themselves to be rented temporarily. These acquired another name: *employees*.

Land as well was owned. Likewise the water, food, and medicine which emerged from the land, and the wood captured in trees which built and heated the homes. On maps made of paper, borders were inscribed. Titles and deeds were assigned. The documents were traded for vast sums of money in spite of the fact that they were merely permission slips to occupy spaces freely given and structures built and paid for long ago.

Once EuroAmericans realized nearly everything necessary for survival could be withheld, they turned their backs completely on the Instructions of the Greatest Great-Grandparent and the universal ethic of care. No longer would they give to the best of their ability nor consume only for their needs. Going forward, the acquisition of money, from a small and apparently shrinking supply—though the numbers continued to multiply—established itself as the one and only motivation. Due to scarcity on one hand, and desire on the other, fear mixed with greed, the pace of consumption quickened noticeably. At least, that is, among those with surplus money.

On one hand, money seemed the silky lubricant which kept society running. Most decisions were filtered through the questions, "How much will it cost?" and "How much can be made?" If answers were either "Too much," or "Not enough," respectively, money magically morphed. It became the gravel in the gears of commerce. For EuroAmericans, to work to care for neighbors without regard for money fell far beyond the realm of comprehension. Numerals, denominated as dollars, a psychological construct with no basis in reality, stopped them dead. Sometimes literally.

With imaginations so calcified, the tragic consequences ramified. Humans were no longer concerned for the care of their elders, neighbors, siblings, and kin. From now on, it was every man [*sic*] for himself. "If others had to do without, so be it. That only leaves more for me," was often heard, then believed. "Probably they deserved it anyway, lazy savages!"

To impose the concept of ownership required a heavier hand of government than earlier imagined. Rulers, formerly steward-managers, now in need of (un)just compensation, procured taxes from the citizens. Additional levies allowed the rulers to dole out privileges to bribe citizen complicity. Under the circumstances, compliance was easily coerced.

New specialties in the divisions of labor had to be created, also requiring (un)just compensation. Warriors, officers, and regulators were selected to enforce compliance. New instructions, called *laws*, told slaves and employees what to do while the Pyramid was constructed, and how to behave during brief periods of rest. At times the bribes and privileges proved insufficient to gain full compliance. In response, regulators were authorized to seize the assets of non-cooperative owners of wealth and property. Seizures were deposited in the rulers' vaults and redistributed to their minions' burgeoning coffers.

For the non-cooperative citizens who owned neither wealth nor property, with the stroke of a pen, rulers changed their status to criminals. Then, the rulers' henchmen, the warriors and officers, could coerce the poor physically. "Mild corrections" were meted out through harsh treatment. If the warriors or officers lost their composure, out of fear or anger, let's say, no need to fret or worry. With the same pen in hand, rulers justified all killings legally. The terrifying message to witnesses and survivors was clearly received.

Physical enforcement was a blunt but effective instrument. Weapons were invented to safely kill humans from beyond arms' reach. Then there were the cages to keep the living locked inside. State-sponsored terror was legitimated through euphemisms like "law and order," military "rules of war," and police "use of force." Private citizens ruthlessly patrolled their right to bear arms. With such imaginative ideas, violence was duly authorized.

EuroAmerican religious leaders, the unlikely co-conspirators of the erectors of the Pyramid, used softer methods to coerce behavior. Thoughts and beliefs were regulated through rituals and messaging. They told a story of eternal torture for the disobedient; eternal rewards for the submissive; and innate sin but grace for the supposedly unworthy.

Rational humans with little to no power solved the dilemma easily: "Better to submit. What's the harm, after all? There is no sense in taking chances that you'll burn later on." Faithful humans obediently followed along. They avoided sin, as the religious leaders had defined it, at least publicly, and welcomed any possibility of grace. The process has been humming along, serving its purpose, with a few twists and turns, ever since.

With notions of property rights and religious thought thoroughly enmeshed, those backed by the privilege of surplus wealth and authority allowed voracious appetites to swell. Henceforth, they were willing, or so they said, to never release the material, energy, and work to meet even the most basic needs. Unless and until, that is, a heftier ransom was paid. In the game of chicken, Economicus knew, self-preservation would cave long before greed.

The ransoms were wildly successful. Owners dictated prices at the maximum consumers could bear. A new concept, *profit*, was enshrined. The only restraints Economicus now faced were the neighbors' habits of consumption and the amount of cash on hand. Soon, however, even these would chafe Economicus' limitless greed.

As a result of the ubiquitous messaging, Euro-Americans came to firmly believe that unless more was taken than was needed, the insatiable Market would be unsustainable. To survive, it must be overfed. The addictions and corruption of inequality had become so pervasive, a simple mathematical contradiction escaped them. Actual sustainability depends on taking not more, but less from what is available.

To increase profits and the upward suction of cash, Economicus became adept at utilizing their neighbors' natural propensity to cooperate. Coordinating specialties and talents allowed for the emergence of economies of scale. Complex systems were organized called *corporations*, reminiscent of the corporeal Beings who comprised them. People who worked together were more productive which could have led to more play, more rest, and more creativity. Unfortunately, due to the dynamic free-market's fierce adaptability, and equally persistent greed to colonize every square inch, the principles of the corporation became as corrupted as the rest of society.

Someone staked a claim of ownership and the embodied corporations were cordoned off for sale. The entities were divided into fractional shares and sold for total sums far greater than any individual could afford. Owners of shares, called *stocks*, granted themselves sole authority to set the rules: Extract as much labor for as little cost as possible while maximizing revenues. All income was collected into silos to increase shareholder value. These silos were later renamed accounts for savings and retirement.

While permitted, owners of wealth could purchase humans on the open market for a handsome, one-time price. Rights to private property were entitled for life—and defended to the death. Afterwards, corporations benefited from the employees' right to be rented temporarily. In exchange, owners of the fractional shares reaped rewards from other people's work. "Put your money to work for you," was a slogan which translated to, "Make someone else work twice as much while you, the prudent investor, retire." The accumulation of wealth allowed a few humans to withhold their gifts and talents while neighbors, burdened with double the responsibilities, worked for marginal incomes pegged to a minimum. Economicus preferred the phrase, "As much as they are worth."

Economicus began to chafe, however, at the hard and fast limits of consumers' minimal cash. If Economicus was to accumulate even larger sums, consumers would have to spend more than they could earn as employees. Motives to increase employee wages, it goes without saying, were not incentivized. Economicus craved a new device to resolve the seemingly intractable conundrum.

Fortunately for hoarders of wealth atop the pyramid, even corrupted imaginations, when rested, function quite well. An idea arose that would arrest the underlings for the remainder of their days. After the untimely demise of Pharaoh's army, slavery fell out of favor. But by other names, it would rise again.

If money, like everything else, could be owned, withheld, and released for a profitable ransom, then it could be lent upon condition of its return. Those who lacked money enough for today would pay a fee, like rent, later called *interest*, for the privilege to borrow temporarily.

Better yet, the rents and interest could continue for perpetuity. Money, in and of itself, was impotent. As an accumulated surplus, it was stagnant and useless. Therefore, the principal could idle anywhere as long as rent, interest, and dividends flowed up and in. If the principal were ever repaid, it would only be reinvested elsewhere.

To logical observers, such an idea—to give large sums now and receive small sums slowly over time— seemed irrational and unsustainable. Economicus, on the other hand, was cunning and prescient. Like dealers in a casino, they knew if enough hands were dealt, and rents sufficiently spread, outcomes would always turn out in their favor. As long as the dealer held the cards, and everyone agreed to play by the rules of the house, the system would work efficiently. Losers paid out to winners. For the sleight of hand, Economicus dealt themselves a lavish cut.

In their time off, acting in the role of consumers, employees were issued money through loans to spend easily and quickly today. Next week, when they returned to work, they would work more hours to try to earn the money borrowed and spent, plus interest, as well as their ongoing needs for today. Saving for an uncertain future? It dangled further out of reach than it had the day before yesterday. As anxiety increased, so did employee retention while their power to bargain declined precipitously.

Borrowers were divided by the owner-lenders into two distinct groups. One they loved to see coming. The other they nearly despised. The preferred group were hoarders like themselves. Ample cash was kept on hand but more was needed to feed insatiable appetites. Due to their preferred status, borrowing from a lender cost less than using their own reserves. Interest rates were relatively cheap. Profits for the lenders were low-risk, almost guaranteed. Due to the low cost and easy returns, in a relaxed manner larger sums were issued for longer periods of time. To sweeten the deal even further, rulers bribed borrowers with a deduction in taxes to accept more from lenders than they might otherwise.

In the short term, however, lower returns had to be made up by someone. The group the lenders most despised were saddled with the costs to subsidize the benefits of the well-heeled. Oddly enough, those with the greatest need were charged higher rates than those with the most ability to pay.

The least preferred borrowers worked for income from owner-employers who paid the absolute least, barely enough to break even—and if possible, less.

Wages were pegged so surpluses were never a possibility. When an unforeseen crisis arose, the employee's minimal pay was insufficient to meet the additional expense. Under the circumstances, they faced an irreconcilable choice: Default on the medical bill, utilities, car payment, or rent? Late fees and penalties, pejorative synonyms for interest, only deepened the hole, and the shame, faced next month.

Due to the deficits between income and expenses, owner-lenders were asked to subsidize the owner-employer's meager wages. Begrudgingly, they agreed. But only on one condition: Those most in need must pay the highest rates. To mollify the shame of any conscientious lender, higher interest rates were readily justified. Those with the greatest need—and often a darker skin or lacking a manly anatomy—were perceived as the least worthy, least reliable, and therefore, the greatest risk.

Into the melee, more frugal, conservative neighbors were drawn. As participants in a ubiquitous system which functioned as designed, the machinations landed on everyone. In their day-to-day expenses as consumers, non-borrowers were asked to pay more. Prices had to cover the insufficient wages of the borrower-employees' present needs plus the debts of yesterday. When non-borrowing consumers returned to work, they too felt compelled to demand more.

Pressure was applied to the owner-employers who passed the burden along to their customers. An upward spiral set in. The phenomenon of competition, a euphemism for opposition, overtook the EuroAmericans. Nearly everyone became the targets of distrust, resentment, and scorn—those who earned less and those who earned more. Only those who self-identified safely in the middle believed no one resented them. Until the inevitable day when the hollowed middle was no more.

At the time, EuroAmericans cheered, until finally they believed: "Free market capitalism! It's the best there's ever been!" Income-producing assets, savings, and retirement funds generated a reliable updraft. Rents, interest, profits, dividends, and regressive tax deductions filled the conduits to suction up wealth from below. These devices withdrew funds from those left with too little and deposited the losses in the accounts of those who already had too much. They siphoned wealth from the poor to the rich, from losers to winners, from the bottom to the top. With no alternatives available, and no imagination for the common good, the colonizers appeared to have won.

Those willing to acquire the most and give the least, as well as to create the greatest harms and deceits, had become the most visible, admirable, and successful, according to the definitions of the EuroAmericans. With the disgruntled quietly mollified in their despair, those with above-average income and wealth refined their self-image with polite informalities—a translucent veil to thinly disguise a shared inequality.

In the short span of their brief existence, the stories EuroAmericans had heard as children, and their experiences as adults, all came into alignment. The inescapable reality was one of competition rather than cooperation; individual salvation rather than collective well-being; piety and suffering in this life for a reprieve of paradise after death; and pity for the poor, scorn for the rich, and an irreproachable but shrinking middle class.

With the aperture of the heart and mind so constricted, everything seemed to fit perfectly. For the EuroAmericans, the fairy tale rang true. Until, only seconds ago, the story took an unexpected turn. At the commencement of the very last minute of the ninety-ninth increment of time, two events converged which might, before all is said and done, toll the death knell.

First, the form of religious thought known as EuroAmerican Christianity lost credibility. As the mask fell away, like chaff from a seed, humans looked to understand the universe in new ways. They derived a new method in which to place their faith and to expand their supremacy. The new method began to usurp the explanations of old. Rational, enlightened EuroAmericans discredited any powers greater than their own.

Experimental science began to probe the Laws of the Universe. Rather than to observe the Instructions as they played out, and to learn from them, scientists adopted a paradigm and worked backwards instead. Conditions were arranged and manipulated until desired outcomes were achieved.

Occasionally, scientists stumbled upon results unforeseen. Subjective explanations were proposed to later test the anomalies. Unlike the leaders of wayward religion, scientists held such explanations with modest skepticism. Diligent attempts were made to prove the explanations false in order to demonstrate the reliability of their initial predictions as well as their unbiased objectivity.

By keen observation and rigorous repetition, as the Instructions played out again and again, the scientists' abilities to accurately predict and craft sound explanations appeared to improve. Their participatory role in the observations, the perceptions one wishes to see, were discreetly ignored. If objectivity was questioned, hubris pushed back rather than humility. If observations diverged too radically from the norm, like guardians of a bulwark called *paradigm*, scientists swarmed.

Novel "discoveries"—like prior discoveries of new worlds with no inhabitants, at least none as civilized as those of the EuroAmericans—were staked as a claim of *intellectual property*. Then, to the highest bidder they were sold. EuroAmericans began to act as if they actually had been granted dominion. According to the new scientific method, they came to believe they could, in fact, control the Laws of the Universe.

A second scientific innovation thrust them further from Life and Love's homeostatic equilibrium. Since the emergence of Life on the unnamed planet, every Being, excluding one, had utilized solar energy exclusively to fuel the work to care for elders, neighbors, siblings, and kin. Due to the unrestrained appetites of EuroAmericans, however, the surplus solar energy to feed domesticated Fire had been thoroughly depleted.

The life-giving forests throughout Europe had been decimated. Still unsatisfied, and knowing no limits, EuroAmericans began to dig caverns in the denuded earth. There they found beneath the soil a third supply of energy. Coal fueled the fires to generate heat as well as the power to move machines.

There the digging did not stop. Soon a fourth supply of energy, a form of liquid coal called crude oil, was found even deeper underground. It was as if, buried beneath the soil, two new suns had suddenly been revealed. Once refined, oil would drive machines to do even more extraordinary things. In the primitive use of Fire, EuroAmericans were unsurpassed. They may yet burn the fuel until the inhabited planet becomes desolate.

Like an ironic catch-22, the first coal-fired machines burned coal to run pumps to extract water so the coal could be mined. Since more coal could be taken than was needed, the excess must obviously be burned. Anything less would be inefficient and unsustainable. Therefore, coal-fired machines were invented to manufacture, by the millions, what humans had once made by hand. Cheap and frequent consumption was streamlined. Matter and energy were converted into greater sums of money for fewer people to hoard. If money could not coerce the solar-powered poor to work for wealthy neighbors in repose, then coal, oil, and machines would perform the work instead. More heat, more output, less protest, less noise.

Due to the increased consumption of energy, from the fruit of the vine, the burning of the brush, and two new suns buried beneath the soil, as repositories of solar energy, the human population soared. Some EuroAmericans saw this as a raging success, a sure sign of their foreordained dominance. Others perceived the spike in population as an unequivocal threat.

With heart-wrenching anguish, those pitiful, thirsty, starving black and brown bodies might coax EuroAmericans to share the resources their noble ancestors had successfully colonized. Or, instead, bear firsthand witness to a species-level genocide. What were the beneficiaries of the inefficiency of inequality to do? For most, the conundrum seemed intractable. In response, they feigned ignorance or denial.

"There is nothing to fear," they loudly proclaimed. "Science and the free market will save us." By "us," of course, they meant those they considered worth saving. Death and destruction were merely the latest market opportunities. Their abiding faith in gods old and new (the Economy, Science, or Religion) was unwavering. They were like a child who plays pretend. If only they believed fervently enough, a voluntary change in behavior may yet be averted.

Among the abundance of what was once freely given to be equally shared, and subsequently withheld from reach, the new phenomena called suffering spread. When a minority were permitted unfettered access to their needs and the privilege, power, and freedom to choose, while others were refused, EuroAmericans wrestled with the philosophical: "Why did God allow such suffering to exist?"

Pain and sorrow from natural disasters and disease afflicted all Beings with no regard for the inequality of wealth or status. Human suffering, by contrast, resulted from their relationships with work and money and how they mediated interactions with their neighbors. Money was both the lock and the key to determine access to medicine, housing, food, education, work, and safety. Malevolent power enlivened corrupt decisions while fear, comfort, laziness, selfishness, or greed motivated the (in)action.

Most human suffering, as a result, was experienced in the regularity of daily life. Relief was readily available, but withheld for profitable ransoms, and only released to those willing and able to pay. For those so addicted to wealth and unwilling to experience life in less luxurious ways? They felt their needs had been met quite well. Why should they change?

Deep wells of religious ink runneth over to try to resolve the riddle. How could God, both all-powerful and all-loving, merciful and just, allow suffering such as this? Intuiting the Instructions emanating through the universe, something seemed amiss, like two left shoes one size too small for the feet. A discrete error had been baked into the question. God did not allow suffering. Humans did.

God has not been idle. Our Greatest Great-Grandparent, the Source of the Instructions for the universal ethic of care, has more than fulfilled their role. Doggedly, It, He, She, They—or We, depending on one's perspective—persists in attempts to gain the attention of narrow minds and hardened hearts. The evidence abounds. May those with eyes look around.

With no laws, weapons, prisons, or private property, all Beings, minus one, act with self-restraint. Elders, neighbors, siblings, and kin give to the best of their ability, to care for each other, and to consume only as they need. They live within the thresholds of homeostasis, of continuity and change, a shared equilibrium of mutual reciprocity. Life and Love waits with patience and hope for Sapiens to listen, adjust, and adapt— milder, modern synonyms for ancient phrases: take heed, turn back, repent!

In the final minute, EuroAmerican Christianity became dubious. Some leaders, plagued by self-deception, seemed hypocritical. With the left hand, they preached Christ's love while the other secretly wielded the power to harm women, children, and neighbors. The institution and its participants seemed more or less satisfied with a status quo far from loving, merciful, or just. As a result, many non-believers cast blame on a Christian god as powerful but apathetic. Or, its opposite, vengeful and cruel. For some, an impotent God must be a figment of weak imaginations. Alas, due to human hard-heartedness, many surrendered religious thought altogether. They jettisoned the universal ethic of care meant to bind the web of Life and Love forever. More reliable directions were sought instead from science, atheism, philosophy, or new-age spirituality.

Rather than God and religion, others, such as the well-dressed anarchists on the political right and the more disheveled brethren on the left, blamed the institution of government, or the nation-state, for our collective suffering. Many more blamed multinational corporations or academic elites. For some, the enemy was the 1%. To point a finger at the bogeyman [*sic*] was far easier than to say, "It is I, it is us, we who are responsible. We must radically change, as individuals, families, and communities, in our places of work and our homes, if we are to survive and flourish together."

Regardless of the evasions and distractions, the Instructions embedded in that tiny mustard seed continue to pulse onward. They will carry on as long as Life and Love persists. Can you hear them? Listen closely. Even a whisper can echo throughout the infinite universe.

We need to see the problem of homelessness as only one end of a spectrum of evil that has the massive subsidies to owners at the other. It is a problem that will be as difficult and painful to solve as slavery. Slavery as an evil shared many of the qualities of the present housing situation—it benefited the wealthy, created an underclass, and denied them human rights. The solution was painful, for abolition often required that slave owners abandon their investment with no recompense. To change our attitudes to housing will be no less of a challenge to us than slavery was for the reformers, not only because institutional evil is hard to recognise but also because so many of us benefit personally from the present situation.

Richard Hilken (1992, 1993) in *Quaker Faith & Practice: The Book of Christian Discipline of the Yearly Meeting of the Religious Society of Friends (Quakers) in Britain,* (1994, p. 23.23)

The Days of Sabbath

ooooo

Here, now, we have finally arrived. Our destination lies before us. It is nearly midnight, on something like the thirty-first of December, of the ninety-ninth increment of time. Our Greatest Great-Grandparent eagerly dances on the cusp of a long-awaited celebration, a centennial some call Jubilee.

We live through the long moment just before midnight. This moment where we have met, where we reside, is known by many names. To some, it is the Present. For others, Eternity. Two linguistic symbols representing one reality. This is to be, forever and always, an eternal time of expectant anticipation, sweet longing, and sublime joy.

Though we live as if in exile far from home, from this one reality we can never roam. In spite of the apparent separations, each contrived within the human mind, we are all, in fact, One: elders, neighbors, siblings, kin, us, the Web of Life and Love.

Little more need be said of the places from where we diverged. Suffice it to say, the places where we have been led are stark disappointments. One point is certain, possibly three. First, the Past is utterly complete. It remains immutable. With us, here and now, Past and Present are inseparably contiguous.

Second, the road map of our history, the breadth and depth of its complexity, is impossible to fully comprehend. As a result, our mental maps are intrinsically incomplete. From our current vantage point, somewhat oblique. The general contours are visible though shrouded in memory's mist. While a shared history connects us all, no two are alike. As with Life and Love, so it is with paradox, replete.

For reasons by now quite easily understood, EuroAmericans adopted a story based more on personal preference than honest humility. Our history, blurred by collective self-centeredness, modified by shame, lacks forthright integrity. Fortunately, the story, as it unfolds, is perpetually incomplete. The opportunity still remains to re-member our way Home. The Jubilee, long underway and well overdue, awaits our arrival patiently.

Third, unlike the Past, its nearest cousin, the Future, remains forever out of reach. By definition, it is continuously beyond the realm of firsthand experience. Any possible descriptions, therefore, are little more than myth or fantasy. Whether fictive tale, magical dream, or a dire forecast, the Future exists only within the human imagination. What takes place between its margins is forever undetermined.

A useful concept, the Future may be, to arrange plans and prepare for movements towards safety, health, and peaceful contentment; a wholeness once translated as *Shalom*. But only the perpetual Present, nestled between Past and Future, emerges in actuality. Only the Present is felt, witnessed, and experienced. With each decision, each interaction, each moment, a new creation arises to shape the divots and contours of one present, eternal reality, to sow the seedbed of our ever-growing history, and plot the trajectory forward.

Our shared experience could be guided by the principles conveyed from our Greatest Great-Grandparent: to harmonize with the web of Life and Love, to live safely within the processes of homeostasis, to give to the best of our ability in our care and work, and to limit our consumption of the material and energy freely given to be equally shared by all. Instead, rather than to migrate, integrate, and protect, our ancestors and their offspring chose to colonize, dominate, and defend. The ramifications of their methods have left us ill-prepared to accept the standing invitation to (re)join the Jubilee. If ever we decide to make our way there, that is.

In the present eternity, innumerable Beings quietly seek a way Home to join the Jubilee. Somewhere, one attempts to transcribe a message, a whispered echo pulsing through the universe across the wholeness of time. Elsewhere a person takes a seat, retrieves a book, reads of old sorrows, and new possibilities. Somewhere else, someone leans away from their desk. Alone, exhausted, unhappy in life as well as in work, they often wonder, "What am I doing here? Is this really it?" At home, upon their bedside table, the same book, one among many, all unread.

Next door, in a deep malaise, someone has bought a ticket seeking an escape in blithe entertainment. Nearby, someone watches the news while savoring dessert. Immersed in the screen, they feel slightly sickened—so much violence, so much poverty. In the next town over, while taking out the trash, someone worries anxiously about the environment. Though the issues seem unrelated, most EuroAmericans ask the same question: "What can only one person like me do?"

Again, the error was baked into the question. Answers went unoffered. None knew of the others, yet the question implied a hope. Someone, somewhere, must share their concerns. Though they knew not by whom, nor what to do, all knew something must be done.

Then one night, by the fireside, a couple broke the silence. They began to reflect. Married for several years, finally considering children, both willingly acknowledged a pervasive unhappiness in their relationship and their work. After children, time together would be more sparse. To friends, they often said money did not drive them. What was left unsaid was how time, work, and money factored so heavily into most of their decisions.

Money was at the root of most of their disagreements, the source of much of their stress. In the precious time off, they tried to thread a needle. Before the real world closed in again, they would find some quality time together. During which, they earnestly pledged, to avoid any topic which might lead to conflicts or discomfort.

Voluntarily silenced for such a long time, they had remained trapped in an inherited predicament. They still had hope, however, if not the freedom, to do some good in the world. Maybe someday one would leave the lucrative private sector and work for a small non-profit. Or they would make their first million, retire early, and turn their attention to helping others. If they had the chance, they hoped to find a more meaningful purpose for their lives.

By the bonfire that very night, together they decided: For the sake of their marriage, for the sake of their life, they would begin a routine Sabbath—a day of rest from commerce. One day each week neither would earn nor spend. In addition, they opted out of attending spaces where earning or spending occurred. Instead, they held Sabbath together in the garden. They ate lunch on blankets in mild repose. They shared relaxed conversations about their hopes. They struggled with their fears. They laughed. They made love. They delighted in each other's presence. They met each other for the first time all over again.

In the weeks and months ahead, over dinners with close friends, the couple shared their Sabbath experiences. Around the feast of ideas, the friends were encouraged and inspired. They took the initiative to practice a weekly Sabbath of their own. Everyone agreed to opt out of commerce, to avoid the acts of earning and spending. But each practiced Sabbath slightly differently. They started simply to see what each might learn. Freedom exercised opened hearts and minds to think with expansive creativity.

As they did, perceptions of the world seemed to alter. For example, the physician told of their neighbor who had described the stress of illness along with the misery of their job. Their spouse was ill, needed doctors, and in-home care they could not afford. The neighbor could neither resign nor care for their spouse because the employer paid for both the health insurance and the desperately needed income. The ailing couple dangled between options irreconcilable.

Just that morning, the physician recalled, they were involved in an argument of intense concern. The physician and their spouse vehemently disagreed about where to take their next vacation: relax at the beach house or embark on an adventure abroad. A realization suddenly dawned. The beach house, the trip abroad, and the time off had all been paid for by the insurance company, the employer, the neighbor, and their customers while the ill spouse suffered at home alone.

While the physician spoke, the real estate broker had a realization as well. When the physician concluded, they shared the story of their nephew who was couch surfing in the home of a friend. That is, of course, when the nephew wasn't under the roof of one of their divorced parents, the broker's closest kin. The broker had realized the recent purchase of a third rental property was three more than the nephew could afford.

The professor quietly sipped a beverage attentively listening. The nephew could not afford rent or save a down payment due to four years of college loans. The loan provider had transferred money to the university to directly deposit in the professor's monthly salary. With funds the nephew had borrowed, the professor had made a handsome deposit on a gem of a property. While the nephew slept on someone's couch, the professor reviewed blueprints of their future dream home.

As others spoke, the banker noticed a disturbing pattern. In times past, people worked to earn *before* they spent. More recently, however, many people had to borrow, then work to pay back what was lent. Credit cards, car loans, education loans, medical bills, and mortgages, if they were so fortunate, not to mention taxes for interest on government debt, had been paid for necessities. Due to the rise in inequality, more money was available for loans from overstuffed accounts of a bank's depositors than from income earned in an employee's wages.

At one time, the banker recalled, EuroAmericans had sought raises and grumbled when the increase was small. Now, however, they sought interest rates they might afford and celebrated when the loss of income was low. For those who had to work and borrow, the trends were alarming. For bankers, depositors, and employers, they were nothing less than charming.

For the friends who gathered to practice the days of Sabbath, the stars suddenly aligned. The dots all connected. The troubles had landed terribly close to home. The time had come to diverge from the corrupted, masculine, colonizing ways of Economicus and the EuroAmericans. One evening someone asked a question no one could rescind, "What are we going to do about your nephew, the neighbor's spouse, and all the others like them? What's more, what will we do about ourselves?"

Historically EuroAmericans had defined who was like them far too narrowly. Everyone was deeply concerned, of course, about the misery of persons of color, Black, Brown, and Indigenous; the poor and the incarcerated; migrants and refugees. Up until then, inequality, housing, public education, and health care had been issues to debate, on occasion, in the abstract, privately, among friends. Under precise conditions, pity might escalate to protest. For a time the issues were taken quite seriously as one adopts a hobby or a fad. Sadly, as happens far too often, hobbies are easily dropped and soon forgotten.

As a result, when the most immediate troubles ceased, neighbors unlike them were cast adrift. Each to his own, as the saying went. More pleasure, comfort, and rest were derived from nostalgic memories than the long-term causes of peace and healing the suffering of inequality. Ultimately, luxury and superiority, self-worth and self-esteem, were prioritized over compassion and remedy. It was as if the ancestors and their offspring had to leave the suffering of others visibly in place in order to feel good—or at least better—about themselves.

During the friends' Sabbath gatherings, another realization became clear. The friends who were more financially well-off had numerous more options, more freedom of choice, but far less courage than their less fortunate peers. Over dilemmas of what to sacrifice they wrestled ceaselessly. A tacky self-image of a privileged status was as difficult to release as an adopted identity. Like any active addiction, when the drug of choice is readily supplied, troubles seem so far away. Yet, to reach the other side of healing, the struggle is invariably worthwhile.

Unsurprisingly, the sacrifices of privilege, identity, self-image, or addiction, for a few, were simply too much to bear. To the faux forms of comfort and entertainment they wistfully retired. Like their ancestors before them, they quietly disappeared.

Fortunately, many in the group were propelled forward by all they had gained. Those with less wealth more easily discovered the middle path to serve and live generously. They no longer felt exhausted or oppressed. There was less frustration and resentment, less scorn, envy, and pain. Routine encounters became like unique adventures abroad. Their spirits felt freer. They laughed more easily. They wept without shame. They found within them a peace, trust, and courage to carry on each and every day. They were savoring a foretaste of the joy of Jubilee!

At one Sabbath dinner, the friends grew ever more adventurous. Someone proposed a challenge—possibly the physician. What was said, no one could forget. First, a bold proclamation, "Heal thyself!" But what came next evoked a hearty yawn. "I have lowered my expenses." So steeped in profit-taking, this hardly seemed radical at all. Then, following the pregnant pause, ". . . in order to lower my income and more freely offer my gifts, talents, and care."

In stunned silence, ears perked up to listen more intently. "Material, energy, and work had been freely given to be equally shared by everyone. Who am I to deny care to many, and to others, sell it for selfish gain?" During the days of Sabbath, they realized the high cost of health care—onerous for the healthy, ruinous for the ill—was the direct result of above-average salaries of employees, like them, throughout the field.

The broker had been quietly contemplating something much the same. Plans were in the works to lower their expenses and own but one home: their primary residence. Never to be outdone, and with the gauntlet raised, they decided to up the ante. Forthwith the broker exclaimed, "My rental homes I'll put up for sale,"—another collective yawn—". . . as far *below* the market rate as I can bear." The nephew, and others like them, could finally afford a home of their own *and* pay off their student loans. They might also land a decent job and hang something beautiful on their bedroom walls.

The professor of economics listened closely. They knew these actions would never be enough. Money was a concept, abstract and inert. In its essence, impotent.

The non-action of not-spending and not-consuming was indeed a tremendous help to lessen the material mined, trees harvested, land destroyed, fuel burned, and pollution to dispose. Furthermore, in their Sabbath practice they had noticed something else. If the gasoline and electricity burned, and the wasted food, were dramatically reduced, the natural processes of the Rooted Ones would graciously replenish the atmosphere.

So the professor spoke up. They asked if the friends could elevate their game. Would they also monitor the electricity and gasoline they burned, the wasted food, meat consumed, and miles traveled by air to lower them as well? In unison, with a full-throated, whole-hearted, "YES!" the challenge was accepted. The friends knew they were finally onto something meaningful!

The friends of the Sabbath gathering developed cohesive bonds and an ease with mutual support. Each person worked at their own pace, and in their own ways, but all moved in one direction. New habits developed to carry on for weeks, months, and, eventually, generations. At times, it seemed so easy, frankly, that they grew a little bored. Seeing how far the race was yet to run, some decided a new challenge must be in store.

In the discussions, they debated what constituted life-giving work. What basic forms of interdependence could we not live without? Good, life-giving, necessary work they sorted into five broad categories. There were firsthand providers and secondary suppliers of 1) nourishment, 2) protection, 3) information, 4) healing, and 5) restoration.

In the first category were farmers, plumbers, cooks, and the like. Those who grew, distributed, prepared, and preserved healthy food and fresh water. In the second category of protection were carpenters, tailors, conflict mediators, and first responders—those who kept bodies and spaces safe. The third category, information, included teachers, journalists, artists, religious leaders, and other messengers for a better life. Healing included doctors, nurses, therapists, and dietitians, and those of a similar ilk. In the fifth category, restoration, were sanitation workers, morticians, barbers, and providers of environmental clean-up and disaster relief—those who transformed disorder into order for general well-being and health.

Many in the group decided to adopt new careers in the life-giving fields with less regard for income and wealth. Where a need existed, they would serve generously. Reciprocity was entrusted to the Instructions woven into the web of Life and Love, in God's economy of Jubilee. This was, after all, the underlying logic of an unregulated free market: Where needs existed, there would be demand. If supply was fulfilled, adequate compensation would be provided.

Such compensation, the friends were fully aware, would not magically appear. "Money doesn't grow on trees," was a childhood lesson they often heard and remembered still. Therefore, total expenses were tallied, every dollar spent, for a year of life and work. The accounting was shared transparently and discussed without pride, shame, or hesitance. They helped each other find the way to lower expenses, lower incomes, and break the addiction to money and wealth.

With the groundwork in their budgets laid, and their work reoriented towards care, the gatherings began to consider where to go from there. As word spread of the benefits of reoriented relationships with work and income, the gatherings expanded to include families, co-workers, and friends. So much so in fact, to maintain trust and familiarity, the multicellular groups had to divide and multiply like the mitosis of single cells.

The new gatherings proposed to organize into associations; to more fully integrate their interactions with the principles of Life and Love. In the marrow of their bones, at a cellular level they knew, the synergy of cooperation and symbiosis would outcompete the novel trends of individualism, selfishness, and fear.

The new entities drew on conventional forms. They were modeled after neighborhood associations, communities of faith, corporations, counties, states, and nations. The first was called the Church of the Emancipation, though it was quite unlike any of its namesake before. Participants in the new associations embodied—in life, work, rest, and play—Life and Love's universal ethic of care.

All members and participants agreed to offer their work to the best of their ability and to consume only what they needed. They cared well for themselves and their dependents while minimizing income and expenses. Revenues were collected and dispersed in such a way that everyone's varying needs were completely met and no one's were exceeded. If total revenues fell short of the necessary minimum, incomes were divided equally.

Then came yet another break with tradition. They informed their customers of the actual costs of products and services rendered. Decisions of how much to pay were left to the well-informed customers. After all, the customers were the true employers. They paid the employees' actual wages. The owner-employers who for so long had dictated prices to customers, and wages to employees, were merely middlemen [*sic*]. They had been ascribed the power to rob Peter in order to pay Paul. In the process, they pocketed more than a little silver for themselves.

Informed and empowered customers with sufficient means were entrusted to cover the break-even cost to keep services sustainable. Those with incomes below the median could give what was affordable. Customers with incomes above the median, or surplus savings on hand, could opt to pay above the break-even to cover the difference. Everyone looked forward to the day when no one was asked to give more because others had so little. Contributions were accepted anonymously, revenues monitored collectively. In this way, no one felt any embarrassment of poverty nor, due to their wealth, felt entitled to special privileges. Everyone's needs, regardless of age, ability, or poverty, were met unconditionally.

To Economicus, allowing customers to decide how much to pay seemed irrational and unsustainable. Such a concept must surely fail. Humans, they believed, were thoroughly self-interested, lazy, and unmotivated except by greed or fear. If given half a chance, humans as customers were innately prone to steal. Economicus' views on human nature may have been a projection of their own shallow self-image. As it turned out, most of Sapiens' offspring were trustworthy, responsible, and fair. Within themselves, most perceived these traits. They hoped neighbors experienced them as such as well. Their true motivations were so intrinsic, they often went unnoticed and unstated; once again, like water to the fish or the forest to a tree.

All who wished to join the emergent associations were welcomed upon request. As they caught the gist of what was being asked to (re)organize their lives, all participants were slowly integrated. No one was excluded or disqualified; antiquated concepts now rendered obsolete. In the meantime, variance was accepted, even necessary within degrees, while everyone worked towards a common trajectory.

In order to implement such unconventional ideas in a hostile economy, and release the psychological baggage of intergenerational inequality, participants put forth the effort to develop and maintain familial intimacy and trust. In the early days of Sabbath, the methods were deceptively simple. They gathered together religiously, come rain or shine, for conversation, spiritual practice, and play. Only later did they develop the rules of order to function as a cooperative entity.

Once the Declaration was made, the initial order of business, the Preamble if you will, emphasized above all else the care of children, elders, and dependents. No longer would families have to first receive an employer's begrudging permission to render care to a loved one in need. No longer would incomes, lives, or livelihoods be placed in jeopardy. From that time forward, the balance of power did shift. Life and Love was once again the center of gravity. Commerce was but a small moon held in its proper orbit.

Parents of young children, like adult children of elder parents, asked each other, "What from me do you need today?" In tandem, family members determined what amount of time would be beneficial to spend together and apart. Throughout the long cycle of the years of a life, families followed patterns like the seasons.

For instance, in a child's earliest years, parents stayed with their children based on the level of their needs and dependency. Likewise, in an elders' later years, adult children were available to care for their parents. Like the solstices, when days are very long and nights very short, time together was prioritized over time apart.

In the decades between life's solstices, parents, children, and grandparents allowed their time together and apart to gradually move towards balance, just as days move towards the equinox. Time apart matched time together so everyone's needs for independence and presence were equally and easily met. No one felt neglected or overworked.

In mid-life, from a balanced center, children, parents, and grandparents had optimum flexibility to meet the needs of their family as well as their community. Then, just as equinox yields to the next approaching solstice, time for adult children with elder parents gravitated towards togetherness. As with the cycles of seasons, so too in the endless ebb and flow of presence and care.

As associations like the Church of the Emancipation evolved, participants moved beyond the fundamentals of a Preamble. They developed a new Constitution akin to a rule of life. If newly embodied entities were to converge to achieve symbiosis in the near term, to maintain homeostasis over the long run, and adaptively evolve in perpetuity, everyone agreed the Constitution must mimic Life and Love's Instructions echoing through the universe.

The new Constitution hearkened back to the universal ethic of care and the early days of good governance. It was kept brief, simple, and flexible. Themes of harmlessness, inclusion, and restoration were its emphasis. Liberty and latitude were enabled by the responsible behavior, self-restraint, and mutual trust of each participant. Divergent ideas, people, and groups would exist together until distinctions faded and gradually (re)blended into One. In the interim, disagreements and conflict were presumed.

If someone's poor choice led to another person's harm, the former seized the first opportunity to repair the damage done. In response to one person's pain, no one else was hurt, humiliated, or harmed. The community did not model behavior they wished to deter. Everyone among them was assumed to want to do what was good and right. No one was treated as if they held an innate, irresistible urge to cause harm.

If, on a second occasion, another poor choice was made, an informal intervention was carried forth. As a jury of one's peers, the intervention was led by two neighbors. One was a person who loved and cared for the offender. The second was the person—or as the case may be, persons—who experienced the harm. The loved one informed the offender of the purpose of the rule. Their neighbor informed them of what happened when it was broken. Consensus was reached on appropriate repairs which the offender expeditiously completed.

When errors were made repeatedly, or when the harm was severe, the community intervened. Options were available from which to choose. One option applied to those who neglected to perform an act which was required. They were sentenced to an immersion experience to learn firsthand the rule's beneficent purpose. Another option applied to those who repeated an act explicitly forbidden. For a period of time, they were sequestered away from the community. During the time of separation, appropriate daily practices of care were performed to expedite reunification. Lastly, if multiple people violated a rule, or if the violations formed a pattern, scrutiny was applied to the rule. In this way, the community could discern if the rule had achieved obsolescence or if its enforcement was selectively uneven.

When the Constitution was implemented, participants found a surprise. With less fear and less shame, adults and children had less urge to speak defensively, less incentive to lie. They felt safe to be vulnerably honest and discuss the choices made. In small circles of truth and reconciliation, hearts and minds were healed; spiritual wounds forgiven. The sense of safety, if it wavered, was quickly and easily restored.

Associations of associations had converged to form communities to live within the universal ethic of care. They committed to organize for the equitable provision of material, energy, and work to care well for elders, neighbors, siblings, and kin. Vocations were chosen to feed, protect, teach, heal, and restore. Everyone was unconditionally cared for. Well-informed customers, comparing their budgets with those of their providers, determined the cost of care. Providers agreed to lower expenses, lower incomes, and to avoid accumulated wealth. Revenues were divided so everyone's modest needs were completely met. If revenues fell short of the threshold, incomes were divided among them equally. As the Instructions conveyed from the tiny mustard seed were integrated more fully, participants came to trust each other and the web of Life and Love. Fearlessly, well-nurtured, in security, they flourished.

Before Sapiens' offspring could be fully liberated and reconciled, one last endeavor lay ahead. By this stage in their evolution, the next step was so plainly obvious, debate and contemplation were unnecessary. To Economicus and the EuroAmericans, on the other hand, the next step would have seemed the most radical, the most irrational of all.

From the systems of wealth, poverty, and inequality, participants exercised the option to divest. For the sake of emancipation, they assigned their homes to a trust. Emancipated homes were exchanged from one occupant to the next for the minimal costs of transfer. Homes were occupied and well-cared for, but rented or sold for profit? Nevermore! Neighbors would no longer be enslaved by decades of debt for permission to occupy the fundamental necessity of a home.

Any wealth, also known as equity, entitled to a deed of permission to the occupant had long been accounted as useless: a psychological gimmick, an entry on a balance sheet, pixels on a screen, like sand in an hourglass, or castles on the beach. Concurrently, more liquid forms of wealth were (re)distributed to those with greater needs. The holders of stock, keepers of bonds, and hoarders of cash gradually reduced savings down to the community's median.

Some manumitted their wealth at the time of death through their last will and testament just as their half-hearted, slaveholding ancestors had done. Those of a more abolitionist strand scoffed at the selfish cowardice. They freed themselves and their surplus wealth as quickly as they could. Emancipation and equality were long overdue. Further delay was simply unacceptable.

While these events were occurring, as one might suspect, the free market did not go quietly. Euro-

Americans and Economicus held firm beliefs in the outstretched, invisible hand of their dynamic pyramid. It had become a symbol by which to orient one's life as one would with any object of worship or devotion. Their economic model had infiltrated their minds, like a belief or identity, as an addiction not easily surrendered. With EuroAmericans and Economicus's faith so deeply entrenched, they were doggedly determined. With the aperture of heart and mind so nearly closed, imaginations had withered. They were fearful of anything other than the dynamic scheme of inequality and suffering.

They made it widely known, they were willing to die—a euphemism for willing to kill—in order to sustain it. Violence had become a means of nobility to hoard their contrived superiority. In their self-image, such strength and conviction made them look and feel better than everyone else. This was the myth of Narcissus stoked to pure whiteness.

Fortunately, a remnant had long kept Hope alive. The web of Life and Love was never meant to be owned and withheld, tortured and abused, ransomed and consumed so destructively. By this time, the majority agreed: Humanity's perennial goal was to lower the median income towards zero. Though absolute accomplishment was mathematically impossible, this was the trajectory to perpetually strive in order to heal the addiction to insidious greed.

This meant, of course, that the half who lived above the medians in income and wealth were expected to strive for *less*. As the community's median declined, everyone celebrated in the good news. With the arrival of Jubilee, the wealthiest had no use for money and the weakest were those who needed so much more than everyone else. In this context, everyone—elders, neighbors, siblings, and kin—could flourish forevermore.

An era arrived when Sapiens' youngest offspring, our greatest great-grandchildren, looked back at the behaviors of their ancestors in stunned disbelief: "How could they have tolerated, much less believed, in the contradictory propaganda of rational self-interest, scarcity, accumulation of wealth, unlimited growth, and unequal prosperity?" Thankfully, the offspring had come to universally agree in a far more reasonable, sober idea: to meet in the middle, to strive for equality.

Jubilee was neither utopia nor a panacea, nor would it ever be. Intrinsic to creative divergence and the freedom to choose, dilemmas and conflicts continued. No longer, however, did humans use the power of inequality—in the forms of privilege, violence, neglect, or fear—to achieve narrow-minded, selfish ends.

Instead, conflicts were approached with curiosity and resolved with words and cooperative actions. Unpleasant stresses simply indicated an imbalance; an event had occurred outside of predictions or mutual reciprocity. To remain within the ethical thresholds of homeostasis, imbalances were forthrightly addressed. At the points of inflection, there may be a strain, a shudder, a slowing before the flowing equilibrium of interdependence was restored.

And so it was: Elders, neighbors, siblings, and kin all remained safe, healthy, and content. Shalom was the eternal norm. Continuity in the midst of change reigned in perpetuity. The universe continued to respire, expand, contract like Spirit, like seasons, like breath. The web of Life and Love on the planet now known as Earth was at-One once again. Jubilee, as it turns out, is an original story without beginning or end.

We have been wrong. We must change our lives, so that it will be possible to live by the contrary assumption that what is good for the world will be good for us. And that requires that we make the effort to know the world and to learn what is good for it. We must learn to cooperate in the processes, and to yield to its limits. But even more important, we must learn to acknowledge that the creation is full of mystery; we will never entirely understand it. We must abandon arrogance and stand in awe. We must recover the sense of the majesty of creation, and the ability to be worshipful in its presence. For I do not doubt that it is only on the condition of humility and reverence before the world that our species will be able to remain in it.

"A Native Hill" in *Art of the Commonplace* by Wendell Berry. (Counterpoint Press, 1969, p. 20)

A Turn To Face Shalom

ooooo

Long before words, a universal ethic of care emanated like a still, small voice throughout the universe. Written translations were unnecessary. There was no separation. No names, no groups, no divisions. All was of One accord. The aperture of hearts and minds remain open that someday humans may rejoin the fold. With profound sorrow, prophets and mystics agree: From our current vantage point, possibilities seem dubious.

Since the ninety-sixth increment of time, multi-cellular Beings on the unnamed planet, now known as Earth, have not experienced anything like ascension or paradise. In fact, through fits and starts, events have been quite difficult. In the short span of four units of time, elders, neighbors, siblings, and kin have witnessed five mass extinctions. Like a remnant, a few among them, including our oldest grandparent, have managed to survive. All stand as testimonials to the delicate fragility and steadfast resiliency of life on planet Earth. Once again, Life and Love replete with paradox.

The sixth mass extinction is well underway. Many innocents have already perished. More will likely follow today. Some have never faced such a calamity. In recorded human history, no Noah has faced such a storm, much less survived, any such as this. The resiliency of Sapiens remains largely untested, completely unproven. As a harbinger of what lies ahead, the brevity of our closest kin, through seasons far less challenging, is far less than favorable.

What should be even more disturbing is that if we do not alter our current manner of living, Sapiens will be the next branch pruned. Due to our willingness to destroy so many threads of the web of Life and Love, we perpetrate the sixth mass extinction. We are the forty days and nights of rain. Capitalism is the Great Flood.

Catastrophe could yet be averted; if we heed the Information flowing through the universe to seek more harmonious relationships with our elders, neighbors, siblings, and kin. Though it lessens with each passing day, time still remains. Our Greatest Great-Grandparent has been quite patient. Regardless of our choices, the good news is clear: Life and Love will carry on, with or without Sapiens.

Our lives, such as they are, are organized around words limned into stories. Generated by the imaginations of ancestors long-deceased, the stories have been handed down, adopted, and enacted by their offspring. Which is to say, by us. The stories are as reliable, creative, and malleable as the human imagination. Such as it is, no more, no less. Our ancestors' stories filter and reflect reality, with varying degrees of distortions and omissions, but they are not reality itself. Some of the most well-known stories go by titles such as God's Creation or The Big Bang; Christianity, Buddhism, or Atheism; Capitalism, Socialism, or Communism; Competition for Survival of the Fittest or A Society of Mutual Aid.

This series of organizing narratives is organized as well. The order helps to see that the stories we enact differ. Sometimes dramatically. Therefore, to state the obvious, during a lifetime, choices must be made. We can choose with intention the stories we live out. Otherwise, our actions comply with choices made by someone else: ancestors long deceased or more recent contemporaries. Excluding situations of imposed dominance, compliance, like surrender, is an easy, lazy choice. But then again, so is dominance. Courage, thoughtfulness, and effort are required to walk the Middle Path.

Regardless of how or when, what we choose becomes the organizing narrative around which we conform our lives. The stories and beliefs provide the lens through which we perceive, interpret, decide, act, and interact with each other. Consonant stories, uniformly shared, in truthful alignment with reality, are barely noticeable. On the other hand, stories which are incongruent, within a single mind, or where two or more are gathered, increase the stress and dissonance. Furthermore, if our stories permit, accept, or encourage harm, to others or ourselves, eventually many will partake in the suffering.

The more fervent the belief in our chosen stories, the more factual their appearance. Hence, the more fervent our belief, the more difficult to distinguish what is actually real from what instead we think should be true. The greater the certainty, and thus the rigidity, the more stressful one's lived experience. The stress is felt most palpably at the junctures where learning could otherwise occur. Rather than sit with humility, reverence, and awe during the demonstrations of continuity amid change, we instead busily craft subjective stories, moment by moment, generation by generation, based on our preferences, biases, and beliefs. Then, we try to live them out as if they were one universal, unambiguous reality.

The trinity of Matter, Energy, and Instructions of the physical universe participates in a story as well. It is, I am, At-One, Ineffable, without Word, or Name. More precisely, the physical-material/energetic-spiritual universe is a story in and of itself. The unified story has been dictated in a language, if you will, which most EuroAmericans have yet to learn—much less to adhere.

The history of past and present is composed of an infinite multiplicity of data points. Their intricacy is far too complex for Sapiens to comprehend. In response, our mental faculties habitually narrow the data to wring some semblance of meaning from select events as they unfold, but only where our attention and interests perceive events to be most meaningful. Those considered meaningless are abandoned to the mist. Alas, the universe does not conform itself to anthropocentric narratives—try, try as we might to force upon it our preferences and limited understanding.

For instance, the universe is a reality with neither beginning nor end. Such notions are contrived conveniences to accommodate the limitations of Sapiens' cognition and short attention spans. The physical-material/energetic-spiritual universe cycles and swoons in long arcs of unending motion. Within this dance, we are mere bundles of surplus solar energy, coalesced into physical bodies, imbued with sublime spiritual consciousness.

You are infinite. You are Spirit. You are breath. A whispered echo of the eternal story. A Divine Utterance. You are a fractal of the totality of the universe. You are an opportunity realized, an event—in action and non-action, in sound, word, and deed. We enact beauty and kindness; selfishness and greed; anger, power, and violence; or laziness, luxury, and neglect. Moment by moment, we freely choose deliberately, impulsively, or passively, for good or for ill, based on the stories we live into and believe. What we bind and what we loose, in Heaven as on Earth.

With this in mind, let us note that humans are the only Beings on the planet who use anything like money, fire, or imagination to sow separation, inequality, and suffering. An imaginative concept called *ownership* is the chosen barricade to withhold needs from one another. Another imaginative concept, *money*, unlocks the gate to facilitate their release. *Fire* is the primitive instrument used to perform more work, at a faster pace, than solar energy alone facilitates. Rents, interest, profits, and regressive tax deductions drain the coffers of the less fortunate. Current standards of commerce generate an inequality of suffering from the inseparable concepts of wealth and poverty. All of which began just minutes ago, in the fractional units of the universe.

The EuroAmerican story of fear, sex, violence, competition, and survival is the propaganda of masculinity run amok. Capitalism is the latest instrument chosen for the unequal distribution of wealth, poverty, privilege, power, and work. These are, if not its stated goals, the logical outcomes. If we continue to live by the ancestors' stories, they lead inexorably to catastrophe.

We could continue to comply with the scripts contrived by EuroAmericans and Economicus. We could instead rage, however briefly, at their paltry story. We could even go so far as to protest, boycott, strike, or die willingly. Alternatively, we could very quietly adopt an ancient story anew which transcends the inherited scripts. Non-harm, care, and cooperation brought the web of Life and Love to its beauty and magnificence. They are the Way of Shalom, the Middle Path home to Jubilee.

Though some may be less than cooperative, even hostile to alternatives, our willingness to preserve, enact, and live into a story which saves the web of Life and Love would be unconditionally beneficial for everyone. If we choose well, persist, and inspire others, one day in the future, a more beneficent story will guide our offspring. The stories of rational self-interest, unlimited growth, and scarcity will become the dust of ancient history.

Our suffering is generated and sustained collectively. For those who directly benefit from the inefficient distribution of material, energy, and work, to alleviate the suffering may at first seem like a grave sacrifice. However, once we are beyond the addictions to wealth and inequality, new relationships with work, money, and each other will not be experienced as such. Indeed, you may be one among many who wonder why we were not living this way all along. I hope you will allow yourself to trust those who have listened closely, blazed a trail, and reached the other side.

This book attempts to preserve an original story which has been echoing for all to hear, for all who listen, for eternity. The Church of the Emancipation is one method, among many, to become at-One with that greater story once again. Consider this little book your invitation and map—however partial and incomplete. We are grateful you have come this far. One generation at a time, like braids in a long cord, if we cooperatively participate and persist, together we will make it there. The Jubilee, what some call Kin-dom, some Heaven, all linguistic symbols for one reality, is the natural order of the universe in the here and now. Please, won't you meet us there?

Be aware. It is not utopia. Pain, illness, and death still occur. Conflict as well. They are simply a part of the process. Unlike here, however, such words hold no connotations of discomfort or fear. In the place we seek, conflict and struggle evoke compassion, curiosity, and creativity from love as plentiful as sunlight, gravity, and air. Indeed, such a place surrounds us this very day. Our arrival is much anticipated. The wedding ceremony has long been prepared.

In light of our brief existence, to speak of such a reality may seem preposterous. We tell ourselves that human beings, central in the loving eyes of God and the universe, among all others supreme, are also innately sinful, selfish, aggressive, and lazy. The evidence, some ardently point out, is abundant. "But not me, of course, not us. Everyone other than us, that is. We are the exceptions. Exceptional even. They got what they deserve, and so did we," is often said, then believed. As if eavesdropping on a secret, under their breath someone murmurs, "So what if we're no different? Better get yours first! No one wants to be a sucker!" You can almost feel the smirk.

The words which define divisions between "us" and "them" are completely arbitrary. Compare any large groups of human beings and you will find more diversity within the group, including EuroAmericans, than between the two. In comparisons with our so-called True Self, we tend to justify the imperfection of harmful behavior and mollify residual guilt with harsh self-judgment for not being more perfect already. Many EuroAmericans stubbornly subscribe to perfectionist, black-and-white, or each-to-his-own ways of thinking, all of which stunt curiosity, learning, and flexible responsivity.

A practice of silence, non-judgment, and simple observation would help us to see ourselves more honestly. When freed of the misperceptions created by the inherited stories, we would see ourselves more clearly. In most hours of the day, most days of the week, most years in a life, the vast majority of humans tend to be astonishingly capable of good, trustworthy, responsible, and loving behavior. We tend to prefer to see ourselves, and to be seen by others, in these ways. Thus we act accordingly. If this were not so exquisitely true, what we have already accomplished would be completely unimaginable. Then, take a moment, if you will, to imagine the expansive possibilities of humans unshackled from violence, wealth, and poverty. But be aware, if you ponder long, the insight might inspire you—and the losses of the past will break your heart.

Even more preposterous is our historical and contemporary willingness to harm members of our own species. From vantage points more sensible than the present day, our behavior towards each other would seem utterly absurd. This is most especially true in the irredeemable losses such as the genocide of indigenous peoples throughout the Western Hemisphere, American slavery, the Shoah (Holocaust), atomic bombs detonated over the citizens of Hiroshima and Nagasaki, a war over political-economic ideologies in tiny Vietnam and, in Iraq, a war based on lies of threats that did not exist.

All of the above were perpetrated by EuroAmericans. All would be considered crimes against humanity, if men of authority were not positioned in roles of mutual accountability. Review by a jury of one's peers has its disadvantages. Among the perpetrators, only Germany's Nazis have been held accountable and an attempt at reparations made.

In addition to these crimes against ourselves, the willingness to so casually accept lesser degrees of violence seems equally preposterous. Some examples include police use of lethal force and psychological harassment; mass incarceration, solitary confinement, and capital punishment; adult violence against children; male violence against women; financial coercion for the daily separation of parents from children; bullying and humiliation of subordinates and peers by persons in authority; and, last but far from least, intergenerational poverty. As a representation of conditions and events, this list is far from complete, but the image conveyed is clear. Arguably, the conflagration of mass psychosis that led to the atrocities listed above overwhelmed abilities to intervene, but these ongoing events are certainly within our power to end.

Furthermore, these lists include only the harms we cause each other, among our own species. They say nothing of the astounding willingness to harm the soil, water, air, and other Beings upon whom we depend to flourish. Whereas the lists above, to the segregated mind, speak of varying degrees of homicide, our treatment of the web of Life and Love more closely resembles a form of mass suicide. The long, slow atrocity might be compared to a fetus attempting to abort its mother from the inside out. A strongly distasteful image—and yet, and yet, so apt.

Lastly, our willingness to harm ourselves leaves the destruction of other Beings on whom we do *not* directly depend to seem so thoroughly acceptable that it hardly merits a mention. Likewise, for any responsibilities we, as a species, may hold towards interdependence—to care for those who would otherwise depend on us—within our own species or others—we live as if oblivious. Sadly, it seems as if we have come to firmly believe that fear, selfishness, and destruction are intrinsic to existence. Such a belief was inculcated by the stories of our masculine ancestry and enacted by their offspring. Where we take them from here is entirely up to us.

Fortunately, good teachers abound. Many live among us and quietly practice here and now. Their examples could guide us to learn the ways to care well for each other and ourselves. Some teachers have departed the physical-material plane. While here, they elucidated a multitude of variations on the universal ethic of care. Their wisdom remains here with us to be practiced each and every day.

The original, eternal story these teachers embody and share is ready to be adopted, lived, and experienced today. Much of EuroAmerican Christianity, on the other hand, has relinquished its responsibility to teach the daily practice of the universal ethic of care. Maybe the Devil, a cunning expert in leveraging growth, endowments, and debts, has gained a hold of its tongue. One day each week its members apply tourniquets to treat the wounded survivors. Then, during the six days to follow, they religiously attend to the accumulation of wealth and the distribution of poverty.

EuroAmerican Christianity has not been highly successful in its ability to exemplify Christ-like behavior. Nor for its ability to guide its flock to live as such. To the contrary, nearly everyone is convinced, by the Church no less, that to live as Christ has asked is well beyond our mortal ability. This is yet another story, contrived by our ancestors, and adopted by their offspring, as if it were factually, unalterably true. To again state the obvious, such ideas imply Jesus's faith in us was incredibly overblown.

On the other hand, EuroAmerican Christianity has been very successful in its ability to attract and retain members, and collect their tithes, in exchange for an eternal promise of life after death determined on a case-by-case basis. In the meantime, until the promise is redeemed, an invitation stands to join a community of like-minded believers with mild demands. The good news, it is safe to say, is that the deceased appear to be 100% satisfied.

Christ did not request a tithe of 10% to leave 90% on the table to spend as one wishes. Life and Love gives itself freely and unconditionally. Paradoxically, it asks for nothing and the same—complete unconditionality—in return. It seeks our whole Being, Body, Spirit, and Mind, as if we were at-One, without division or separation, so that we may love and be loved in return. Yet for the EuroAmericans to "sell everything you own and give it to the poor" seems at least as daunting as to "love your enemies." And so we continue to live as if in exile far from home, as a bird with wings who never thought to fly, or was persuaded not to try.

All material and energy have been freely given to be equally shared by all. Therefore, we could freely give of our work, service, and care to the best of our ability. No one need be disqualified from participation. If offered willingly, everyone's efforts would be graciously received. Our needs to thrive should never be withheld, especially due to age, ability, or poverty. Only the complete minimum of material and energy should be taken and consumed. Care for our children, elders, and dependents should be prioritized above employers, shareholders, and the so-called free market economy.

Reciprocity, interdependence, and mutual flourishing could guide our decisions, in contrast to individual selfishness, the accumulation of wealth, privilege and power, violence and aggression, or laziness and luxury. Our interactions could demonstrate practices of care, responsibility, self-restraint, trust, courage, and faith. Choices are small—each and every moment, each and every day, one generation to the next. Best of all, the choices are ours to make.

Until the Body of Christ again finds its voice to lead by example, with and without its words, inspiration might emerge from smaller entities: one person, one family, one friendship circle, one community at a time. Movements arise voluntarily. Personal decisions determine the method and the time. Otherwise, we wait for a government fiat or an undeniable catastrophe.

Sooner rather than later is an imperative of many mystics, prophets, teachers, and survivors. Obviously, not everyone agrees. Some clearly prefer to wait until they are told, "Come, this way. Yes, now. Follow obediently, please." Others wait as well, but for the day when they hold the power to tell others when and what to do.

If we all moved toward one destination—let's name it Shalom—arrivals would naturally flow from diverse directions and at differing speeds. Our circumstances vary person to person, family by family. If we travel too cautiously, the status quo will be preserved too long. Prior to arrival, Life would cease. If we travel too hastily, unforeseen harms ensue and expedite the destruction. In the incremental middle, calibrations alleviate stress through patience, trust, and equanimity.

Pardon the redundancy, but it can't be said enough: Care for our children, elders, and those dependent upon us must be prioritized, over and above any owner or employer, first and foremost. Building shareholder equity, accumulating wealth, and private property should never have taken priority over care for children, elders, and dependents. Current priorities are a holdover of the hierarchy of EuroAmerican masculinity. The consequences have been a profound travesty. In the near term, as consumers, we will need to adjust our expectations and patterns of consumption rather than to ask our children, dependents, and elders to continue to sacrifice on behalf of our privileges and convenience.

A humble suggestion to begin: start small. Develop routine practices to care well for ourselves. Healthy food, ample sleep, and ongoing learning would be a nice beginning. Moving outward, we can practice better care within our relationships, homes, and environment. Burn less electricity and gasoline, travel fewer miles by airplane, waste no food, and eat less meat. Apply effort and energy toward work and careers more necessary and life-giving than lucrative in pay and benefits. Lower expenditures as much as possible; first in entertainment, collectibles, and all of the new and unnecessary stuff. Then, and more importantly, lower payments to rents, debts, and insurance. These practices facilitate the reduction in incomes so that access is more affordable for everyone. If personal income has reached the community's median, when you are able, go lower. Please put your shoulder to the plow and pull!

Finally, when you are ready, begin to divest excess savings to the lowest levels which feel safe; based on your age, the progress to emancipate yourself from the addictions to money, and our progress to meet your needs more freely. To gauge the timing, the early signs will first be noticed internally. More often you will feel trust and contentment as they displace fear, anger, and anxiety. Relationships will be more reliable; isolation, a fading memory.

Externally, you will start to notice housing, health care, and healthy food become more easily affordable and available. People will speak less of increasing income, exorbitant prices, and the financial value of their property. Divestments will be generously distributed to relatives, neighbors, or strangers with savings below the median. Consider these distributions as reparations without the interminable wait on partisan legislators.

You may be surprised to learn who is the intended audience for this book. It was not written to indulge the left-wing progressives who rail vociferously against systems of oppression, power, and wealth. No purpose is served by preaching to the choir—assuming, of course, that the choir has reorganized their relationships with consumption, money, and work. Otherwise, as humans are wont to do, we may find that members of the choir simply point fingers and cast aspersions at disembodied systems. They hope the culprits will see the light, mourn their errors, and lead the way to repentance.

In addition, when the solutions are left to recalcitrant culprits, we render ourselves small and powerless. Likewise, we mire down in a mud of our own making if we assume roles of oppressed victim with no imagination for routes of escape. Disembodied systems in need of change are comprised of human beings similar to ourselves. Their minute decisions, interactions, and relationships follow similar scripts. If the scripts which equate security with monetary wealth were rendered meaningless, Maleficence would be neutered into impotence.

If you happen to live near the so-called margins, please do not strive to be more like the wealthy and powerful who over-consume and destroy. Instead, as you are able, offer your ways to inspire and lead for the sake of freedom and generosity. You are closer to the Jubilee than you may realize, and certainly much closer than many have believed heretofore. By the EuroAmericans' stories, we've all been deceived. You are the overwhelming majority. The self-centered minority must learn to come towards you.

Therefore, we hold ourselves personally responsible to alter our relationships with money, work, and consumption in the home, workplace, and communities. Then inspire others to adopt practices to care for the whole of the web of Life and Love. The looming flood called capitalism cannot be overcome while we try to maximize income, save for retirement, insure against unaffordable losses, and borrow enormous debts.

This book, as you may have deduced, does not intend to win mass approval nor gain popularity. In fact, the audience for whom this book was written should be the most discomfited. To avoid any confusion or evasion, allow for this specificity: If you are among the 133 million people who reside in the United States, with an annual income between $70,000 and $200,000, and/or a net worth (retirement savings and property) in the black, this book was written for you. The more "successful" and the younger you are, please rise. We have empty seats in front.

You are the 40% who provide the buffer which keep current systems functioning. Without your co-operation, such steep inequality and suffering would cease. The 50% below the median would rarely have their needs denied. In addition, the conduits to siphon wealth to the uppermost 10% would leak, then dry up. If you are among the upper 10% with your hand on the spigot and buckets to overflowing, you are welcome to join us. When the front row is down to one seat left, your name will be on it and the door will always be open.

This book also addresses persons in positions of authority, whether in the home or our places of work. If you have the privilege and power to make decisions which affect the lives of others—such as children, customers, employees, tenants, migrants, prisoners, and citizens—you can continue to conform to the old scripts. You could continue to operate according to the harmful notions of the accumulation of wealth and inequality. Or you might put into practice more loving methods for an efficient distribution of material, energy, and work; all of which was freely given to be equally shared by us all.

Lastly, this book is written for those who generate the narratives we organize our lives around: faith leaders, economists, scientists, journalists, artists, teachers, and others. The ideas we espouse, and the words we put forth, create perceptions, expectations, and experiences one utterance at a time. The scripts collectively enacted emerge from the words we choose and demonstrate with silent integrity.

You are being asked to mindfully guide us in new directions. We wish to move away from the notions of individualism, wealth, and scarcity. Instead, help us to comprehend, embrace, and move towards reciprocity, equality, and flourishing. Your assistance is much needed and greatly appreciated.

As a form of motivation, discomfort is extraordinarily helpful. If a path to relief is explicitly known, and hope exists that comfort is within reach, most humans will hardly rest until comfort is achieved. Contentedness is our preferred baseline state of existence. The hope of prophets and mystics alike is that some of the reading audience are so perturbed off-center that they must recalibrate to find a new equilibrium.

In conclusion, let us consider one last story often told. It addresses the question, "Who are we, innately, as individuals, as a species, down in our souls?" If we were to imagine ourselves raised without the corruptions of the human economy and the narratives that our lives have been organized around, what would we, as a species, be like? At our spiritual-energetic center, as individuals, who would we be?

To say we are innately "good" is far too vague. Like normal, weird, sinful, and bad, this adjective has become rather meaningless. Good persons, good schools, good neighborhoods, and good jobs all denote success at conformity with the scripts which perpetuate great harm. Being "good," like "nice," may be the near enemy of Shalom—weak substitutes which surreptitiously undermine the actualization of wholeness, peaceful contentedness, and equality.

On one hand, the good people who so politely adhere to the scripts handed down, who on occasion advocate for those less fortunate, make inequality and injustice difficult to uproot. Possibly more so than the outwardly selfish and cruel. A meager 10% in charity upholds the stability of the status quo. Mild, temporary relief, for which we are grateful, but no fundamental change in one person's misfortune or another's luxury.

On the other hand, the selfish and cruel minority who unabashedly revere inequality and superiority stifle Beneficence. They choose instead to organize around ideas of masculinity, private property, American exceptionalism, and white supremacy. When they attempt to justify, defend, and explain away clearly harmful, unjust ideas, attitudes, and behavior, matters are only made worse, not better. At least, it is no secret for whom they stand. They stand for themselves and little else.

Instead, I ask you, "Are we innately selfish, aggressive, lazy, or neglectful? Including or excluding people like yourself?

"If untended and uncultivated, do we go wild, spread like weeds, or wither? What happens if we are neglected and our needs are withheld? What happens to those who do the withholding?

"What happens if we are yelled at, frightened, humiliated, punished, and abused? What happens if such attitudes are doled out by strangers? By people we love? Or those who are supposed to love us? Who or what do we become?

"If we are well cared for and attended to, if our needs for presence and sustenance are readily met by loved ones, neighbors, and the community, do we then become people of integrity, trustworthy, responsible, and kind?

"What if we allowed ourselves to finally see that Life and Love was like sunlight, gravity, and air, that all material and energy have been freely given to be equally shared?"

The answers are left to you to decide.

> "We're a race of Jeremiahs, prophets calling for the nation to repent."
>
> "Exactly!" Geneva said. "And you know what nations do to their prophets?"
>
> "I do. About the least dire fate for a prophet is that one preaches, and no one listens; that one risks all to speak the truth, and nobody cares."

Faces at the Bottom of the Well: The Permanence of Racism by Derrick Bell. (Basic Books, 1992, p. 157)

Acknowledgments

ᴏᴏᴏᴏᴏ

First and foremost, I wish to thank all those who read and recommended my first book, *A Quiet Revolution of the Heart* (2021). Without you, and those who supported it financially, I would not have believed it worthwhile to try again.

Secondly, I want to thank those who offered polite, yet terse compliments or silent disapproval of that first work. Without you, I would not have been inspired to write *Jubilee*. You spurred me to attempt something better.

My deepest gratitude I wish to extend to those who contributed to bringing this work to fruition. The teachers whose wisdom was poured into *Jubilee* are far too numerous to mention. From the Hebrew Prophets, Lao Tzu, Siddhartha, and Jesus of Nazareth to the many scholars, historians, poets, activists, and mystics in our modern day. Not a word contained herein could have been written without them.

Personal thanks go to Laura Bardolph of BBH Literary for her fastidious editorial attention; to Della Chambless for the thoughtful suggestions she made of a late draft of the manuscript; and to Lydia Hall for turning a plain manuscript into a beautifully designed book worthy to be held by your gaze. You all demonstrate firsthand that mutual trust, cooperation, and interdependence are integral to achieving every innovation we put forth.

Lastly, I'd like to thank you, dear reader for choosing to read, and hopefully to practice, the ideas passed down to us. Without you, all of the efforts of those above would be for naught. We offer to you many blessings and much love.

Appendix of Luminaries

ooooo

So I have spent my life watching, not to see beyond the world, merely to see, great mystery, what is plainly before my eyes. I think the concept of transcendence is based on a misreading of creation. With all respect to heaven, the scene of miracle is here, among us. The eternal as an idea is much less preposterous than time, and this very fact should seize our attention. In certain contexts the improbable is called the miraculous.

> From *The Death of Adam: Essays on Modern Thought* by Marilynne Robinson. (Picador, 2005, p. 243)

ooooooooooooooo

No matter what goes missing, the object you need or the person you love, the lessons are always the same. Disappearance reminds us to notice, transience to cherish, fragility to defend. Loss is a kind of external conscience, urging us to make better use of our finite days. Our crossing is a brief one, best spent bearing witness to all that we see:

honoring what we find noble, tending what we know needs our care, recognizing that we are inseparably connected to all of it, including what is not yet upon us, including what is already gone. We are here to keep watch, not to keep.

From *Lost & Found* by Kathryn Schulz. (Random House, 2022, p. 236)

I do not wish to suggest that there are not many who are participating in the social struggle inspired to do so by deep religious convictions. But my insistence is that the church has lost the initiative to inspire such behavior in our society. The image of the church is so damaged that at the moment it does not provide an effective rallying point.

From *The Luminous Darkness: A Personal Interpretation of the Anatomy of Segregation and the Ground of Hope* by Howard Thurman. (Harper & Row Publishers, 1965, p. 21)

Even more importantly, and publicly, we may all begin to understand religion as being a very truly compassionate expression of the great human "longing" for participation in the wholeness of the universe. Thus we may absorb more fully Gandhi's equation of the religious quest with the search for truth. We can explore with our classes the religion of the Hebrew prophets, hear the powerful announcement that true religion consists of love for God and humanity, that true love leads to service, especially to the poor, the weak, and the oppressed. They may look through the window of the Black freedom movement and discover a religion beyond buildings and institutions that is a profound personal and collective recognition of the oneness of humankind. They may see that religion is the commitment to give our best self to the work of nurturing and defending the great connectedness, through personal disciplines, collective work, and public witness.

> From *Hope and History: Why We Must Share the Story of the Movement* by Vincent Harding. (Orbis Books, 2nd ed, 2009, p. 73)

ooooooooooooooo

Research along these lines may well be underfunded. The Sabbath has a way of doing just what it was meant to do, sheltering one day in seven from the demands of economics. Its benefits cannot be commercialized. Leisure, by way of contrast, is highly commercialized. But leisure is seldom more than a bit of time ransomed from habitual stress. Sabbath is a way of life, one long since gone from this country, of course, due to secularizing trends, which are really economic pressures that have excluded rest as an option, first of all from those most in need of it.

> From *The Givenness of Things: Essays* by Marilynne Robinson. (Farrar, Straus, and Giroux, 2015, p. 115)

A colonial ruler does not just want the natives to bow down and render obeisance to their new sovereign. The natives must also grow food, pay taxes, go to work in mines and on estates, provide conscripts for the army, and help to hold the line against rival powers. For these activities to proceed, the natives must not just submit, they must cooperate.

> From *Racecraft: The Soul of Inequality in American Life* by Karen E. Fields and Barbara J. Fields. (Verso Press, 2012, p. 138)

The British colonial rulers of India were more intent on ensuring the smooth workings of the "free market" and their colonial revenues than in preventing famine and death by starvation or disease. There, people died in sight of wheat being loaded onto railroads destined for consumption in Britain, and the colonial authorities spurned famine-relief in the belief that it weakened "character" and promoted sloth and laziness.

> From *The Origins of the Modern World: A Global and Ecological Narrative from the Fifteenth to the Twenty-first Century* 2nd ed, by Robert B. Marks. (Rowman & Littlefield Publishers, Inc. 2007, pp. 148–149.)

The problem is that they are unable to find anyone determined enough to carry out this revolution, with the result that they become bitter, sceptical, passive, and ultimately apathetic—in other words, they end up precisely where the system wants them to be.

> From *Living in Truth* by Václav Havel, ed by
> Jan Vadislav. (Faber & Faber, 1990, pp. 92–93)

∞∞∞∞∞∞∞∞∞∞∞

Habitual actions, feelings, and thoughts come "naturally"—that is, they require little attention and involve no unaccustomed physical, emotional, or mental exertions. Change the pattern, however, by introducing novel activity, feeling and thought, which require attention, study, learning, and the individual resents the innovation and demands freedom to follow his habitual lines of conduct. "Free" in this case, means an escape from the inconvenience, awkwardness, and annoyance which go into every learning process. The slave to habit asks freedom to continue in his slavery.

> From *Man's Search for the Good Life* by Scott
> Nearing. (Social Science Institute, 1954, p. 17)

∞∞∞∞∞∞∞∞∞∞∞

I have found that, to make a contented slave, it is necessary to make a thoughtless one. It is necessary to darken his moral and mental vision, and, as far as possible, to annihilate the power of reason. He must be able to detect no inconsistencies in slavery; he must be made to feel that slavery is right; and he can be brought to that only when he ceases to be a [hu]man.

> From *Narrative of the Life of Frederick Douglas: An American Slave written by himself, 1845* (Penguin Books, 1994, pp. 83–84)

oooooooooooooooo

Mrs. Luke said, "Ruby [Bridges] was 'a deep child,' and added a terse afterthought: 'I hope she doesn't suffer later. The more you think and the deeper you are, the more you feel.'"

> From *Women of Crisis: Lives of Struggle and Hope* by Robert Coles and Jane Hallowell Coles. (Merloyd Lawrence Book, 1978, p. 4)

oooooooooooooooo

She should know. She doesn't go throwing big fat checks at her "help." She's "fair"; she keeps on reminding us—but she's not going to "liberate" us, anymore than the men are going to "liberate" their wives or their secretaries or the other women working in their companies. That's the world for you. Look at our Lord, Jesus Christ—all the trouble He had, trying to convince people to be nicer to each other, and share their riches with the poor, and be equal before God. They killed him for talking like that!"

> From *Women of Crisis: Lives of Struggle and Hope* by Robert Coles and Jane Hallowell Coles. (Merloyd Lawrence Book, 1978, pp. 266–267) [the person quoted is Helen, a factory worker from the Piedmont of North Carolina]

∞∞∞∞∞∞∞∞∞∞∞∞

Well, if one really wishes to know how justice is administered in a country, one does not question the policemen, the lawyers, the judges, or the protected members of the middle class. One goes to the unprotected—those, precisely, who need the law's protection most!—and listens to their testimony. Ask any Mexican, Puerto Rican, any black man, any poor person—ask the wretched how they fare in the halls of justice, and then you will know, not whether or not the country is just, but whether or not it has any love for justice, or any concept of it. It is certain, in any case, that ignorance, allied with power, is the most ferocious enemy justice can have.

> From *No Name in the Street* by James Baldwin. (Vintage Books, 1972, pp. 148–149)

These are facts which are neither denied nor acknowledged but are met with an unbreakable conspiracy of silence—because to deny them would be too obviously absurd and to acknowledge them would condemn the central preoccupation of modern society as a crime against humanity.

> From *Small is Beautiful: Economics as if People Mattered* by E. F. Schumacher. (Harper Colophon Books, 1973, p. 35)

ooooooooooooooooo

The plain truth is, the continuation of this system is a sin; and the sin rests upon us: It has been eloquently said that "by this excuse, we try to throw the blame upon our ancestors, and leave repentance to posterity."

> From *An Appeal in Favor of That Class of Americans Called Africans* by Lydia Maria Child, pub 1833, edited by Carolyn L. Karcher. (University of Massachusetts Press, 1996, pp. 70–71)

Very well, thought I: "Knowledge unfits a child to be a slave." I instinctively assented to the proposition; and from that moment I understood the direct pathway from slavery to freedom.

> From *Narrative of the Life of Frederick Douglas: An American Slave written by himself, 1845* (Penguin Books, 1994, pp. 217–218)

oooooooooooooo

I had my secret hopes; but I must fight my battle alone. I had a woman's pride, and a mother's love for my children; and I resolved that out of the darkness of this hour a brighter dawn should rise for them. My master had power and law on his side; I had a determined will. There is might in each.

> From *Incidents in the Life of a Slave Girl, Written by Herself* by Harriet Jacobs, originally published 1861, edited by Nell Irvin Painter. (Penguin Books, 2000, p. 95)

Living within the lie can constitute the system only if it is universal. The principle must embrace and permeate everything. There are no terms whatsoever on which it can coexist with living within the truth, and therefore everyone who steps out of line denies it in principle and threatens it in its entirety.

> From *Living in Truth* by Václav Havel, ed by Jan Vadislav. (Faber & Faber, 1990, p. 56)

ooooooooooooooo

A better system will not automatically ensure a better life. In fact the opposite is true: only by creating a better life can a better system be developed.

> From *Living in Truth* by Václav Havel, ed by Jan Vadislav. (Faber & Faber, 1990, p. 71)

I hope some will buy my books from charity; but I am no beggar. I am now entirely destitute of property; where and how I shall live I don't know; where and how I shall die I don't know; but I hope I may be prepared. If it were not for the stripes on my back which were made while I was a slave, I would in my will leave my skin as a legacy to the government, desiring that it might be taken off and made into parchment, and then bind the [C]onstitution of glorious, happy, and free America. Let the skin of an American slave bind the charter of American liberty!

From *Life of William Grimes, the Runaway Slave, Brought Down to the Present Time, Written by Himself,* New Haven: Published by the Author, 1855, edited by William L. Andrews and Regina E. Mason. (Oxford University Press, 2008, p. 103)

∞∞∞∞∞∞∞∞∞

. . . Our immediate emancipation means, doing justice and loving mercy today—and this is what we call upon every slaveholder to do.

I have seen too much of slavery to be a gradualist. I dare not, in view of such a system, tell the slaveholder, that "he is physically unable to emancipate his slaves." I say he is able to let the oppressed go free, and that such heaven-daring atrocities ought to cease now, henceforth and forever. Oh, my very soul is grieved to find a northern woman thus "sewing pillows under all arm-holes," framing and fitting soft excuses for the slaveholder's conscience, whilst with the same pen she is professing to regard slavery as a sin. "An open enemy is better than such a secret friend."

Hoping that thou mayest soon be emancipated from such inconsistency, I remain until then, Thine out of the bonds of Christian Abolitionism. —A. E. Grimké

From *On Slavery and Abolitionism* by Sarah & Angelina Grimké. (Penguin, 2014, p. 249)

But Sojourner is an old body, and will soon get out of this world into another, and wants to say when she gets there, "Lord, I have done my duty, I have told the whole truth and kept nothing back."

From *Narrative of Sojourner Truth; A Bondswoman of Olden Time, With a History of Her Labors and Correspondence* orig. pub. 1850 ed. by Nell Irvin Painter. (Penguin Books, 1998, pp. 162–163)

ooooooooooooooo